[redacted]

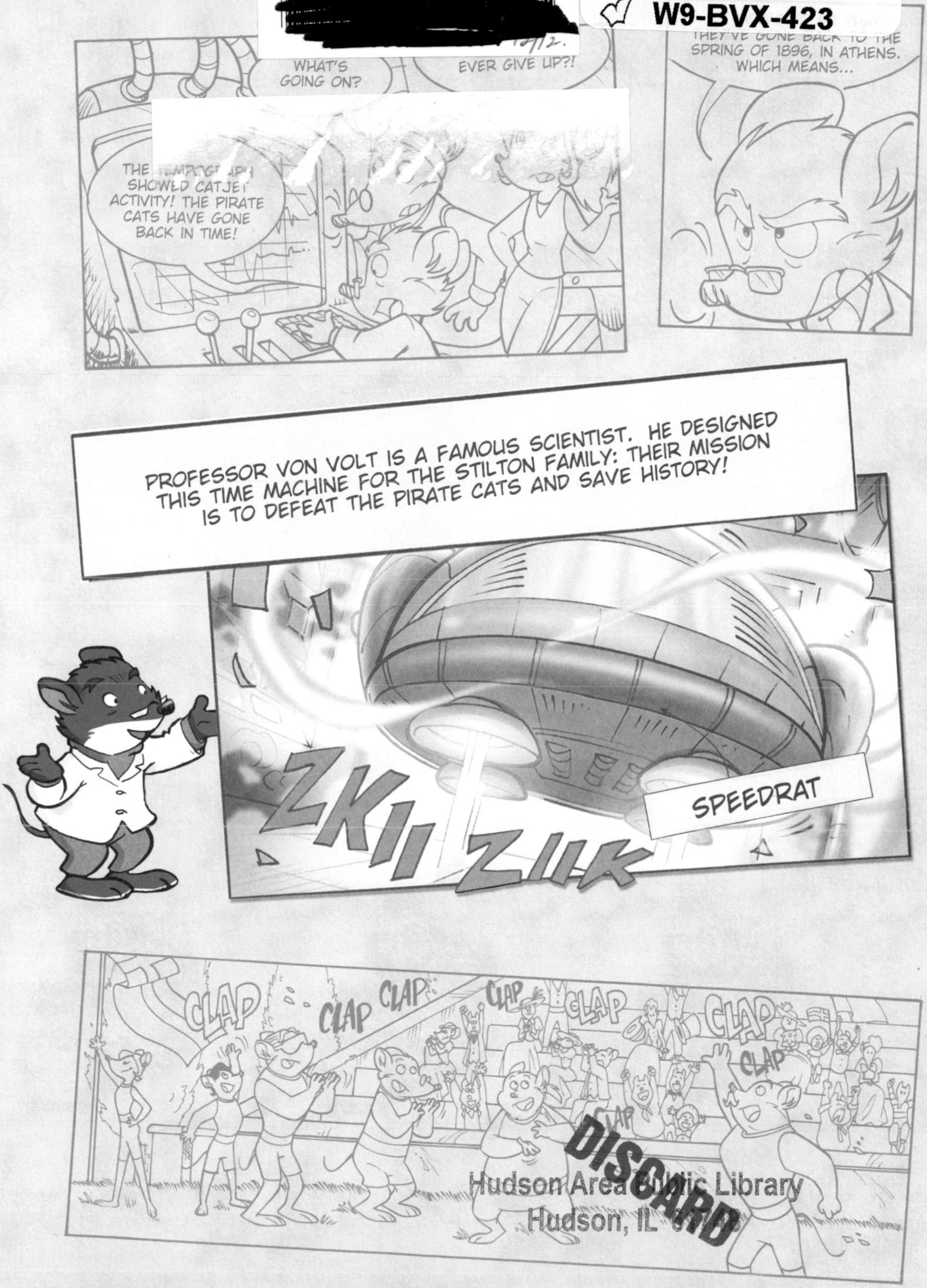
WHAT'S GOING ON?
EVER GIVE UP?!
THE TEMPOGRAPH SHOWED CATJET ACTIVITY! THE PIRATE CATS HAVE GONE BACK IN TIME!
THEY'VE GONE BACK TO THE SPRING OF 1896, IN ATHENS. WHICH MEANS...
PROFESSOR VON VOLT IS A FAMOUS SCIENTIST. HE DESIGNED THIS TIME MACHINE FOR THE STILTON FAMILY: THEIR MISSION IS TO DEFEAT THE PIRATE CATS AND SAVE HISTORY!
ZKII ZIIK
SPEEDRAT
CLAP CLAP CLAP CLAP CLAP CLAP CLAP CLAP

Geronimo Stilton

GERONIMO STILTON
SAVES THE OLYMPICS

PAPERCUTZ™

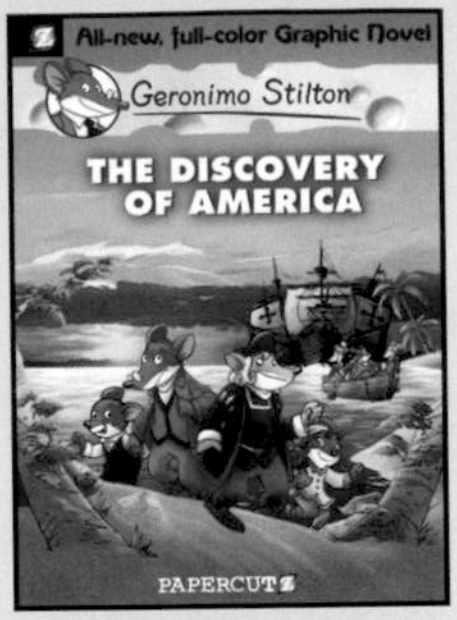

All-new, full-color Graphic Novel
Geronimo Stilton
THE DISCOVERY OF AMERICA
PAPERCUTZ

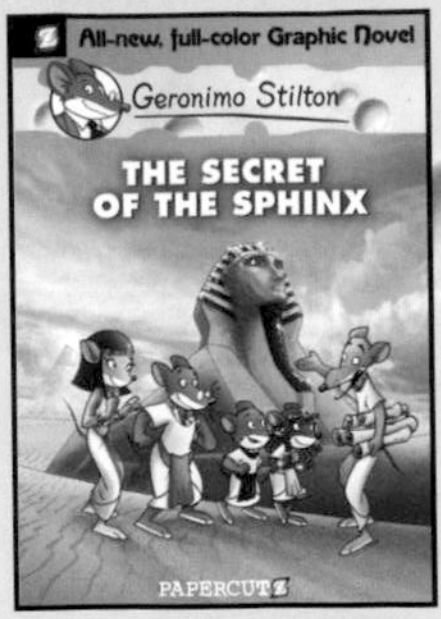

All-new, full-color Graphic Novel
Geronimo Stilton
THE SECRET OF THE SPHINX
PAPERCUTZ

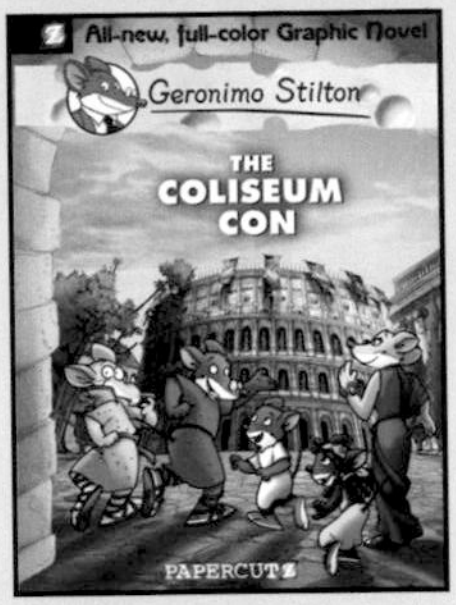

All-new, full-color Graphic Novel
Geronimo Stilton
THE COLISEUM CON
PAPERCUTZ

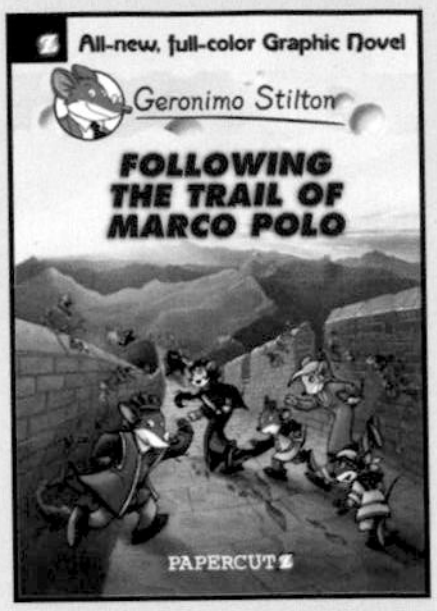

All-new, full-color Graphic Novel
Geronimo Stilton
FOLLOWING THE TRAIL OF MARCO POLO
PAPERCUTZ

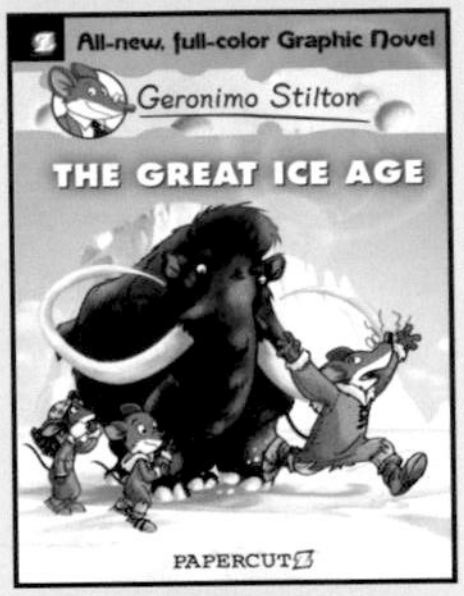

All-new, full-color Graphic Novel
Geronimo Stilton
THE GREAT ICE AGE
PAPERCUTZ

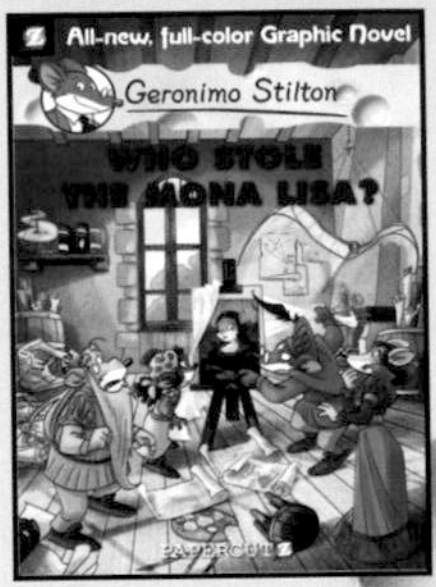

All-new, full-color Graphic Novel
Geronimo Stilton

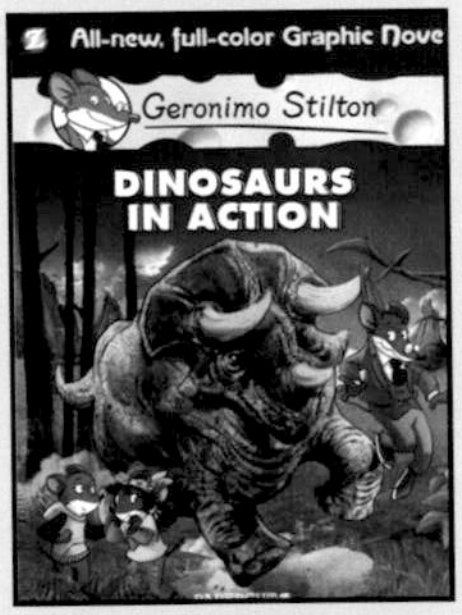

All-new, full-color Graphic Nove
Geronimo Stilton
DINOSAURS IN ACTION

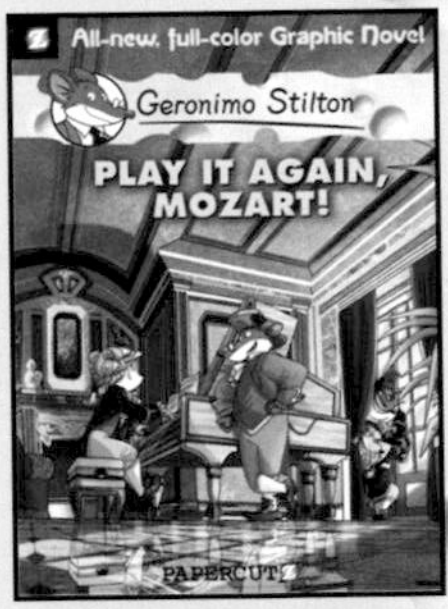

All-new, full-color Graphic Novel
Geronimo Stilton
PLAY IT AGAIN, MOZART!

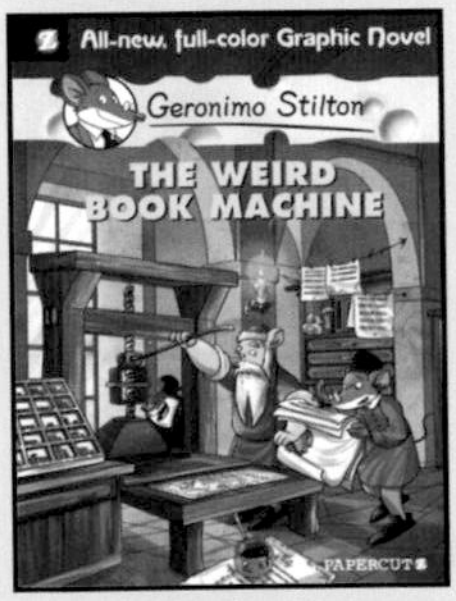

All-new, full-color Graphic Novel
Geronimo Stilton
THE WEIRD BOOK MACHINE

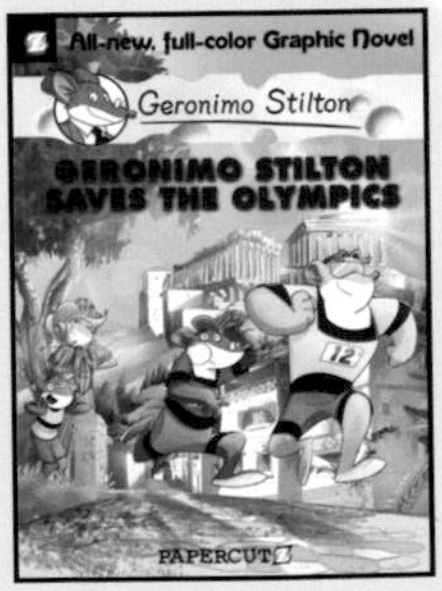

All-new, full-color Graphic Novel
Geronimo Stilton
GERONIMO STILTON SAVES THE OLYMPICS
PAPERCUTZ

Geronimo Stilton

GERONIMO STILTON SAVES THE OLYMPICS

By Geronimo Stilton

PAPERCUTZ™

New York

GERONIMO STILTON SAVES THE OLYMPICS
© EDIZIONI PIEMME 2012 S.p.A.
Tiziano 32, 20145,
Milan, Italy
Geronimo Stilton names, characters and related indicia are copyright,
trademark and exclusive license of Atlantyca S.p.A.
All rights reserved.
The moral right of the author has been asserted.

Text by Geronimo Stilton
Editorial coordination by Patrizia Puricelli
Script by Leonardo Favia
Artistic coordination by BAO Publishing
Illustrations by Federica Salfo and color by Mirka Andolfo
Cover by Lorenzo Bolzoni and effeeffestudios
Based on an original idea by Elisabetta Dami

© 2012 – for this work in English language by Papercutz.

Original title: "Hai Salvato Le Olimpiadi, Stilton!"

Translation by: Nanette McGuinness

www.geronimostilton.com

Stilton is the name of a famous English cheese. It is a registered trademark of the
Stilton Cheese Makers' Association. For more information go to www.stiltoncheese.com

Lettering and Production by Ortho
Michael Petranek – Associate Editor
Jim Salicrup
Editor-in-Chief

ISBN: 978-1-59707-319-6

Printed in China
May 2012 by WKT Co. LTD.
3/F Phase 1 Leader Industrial Centre
188 Texaco Road, Tsuen Wan, N.T.
Hong Kong

Distributed by Macmillan
First Papercutz Printing

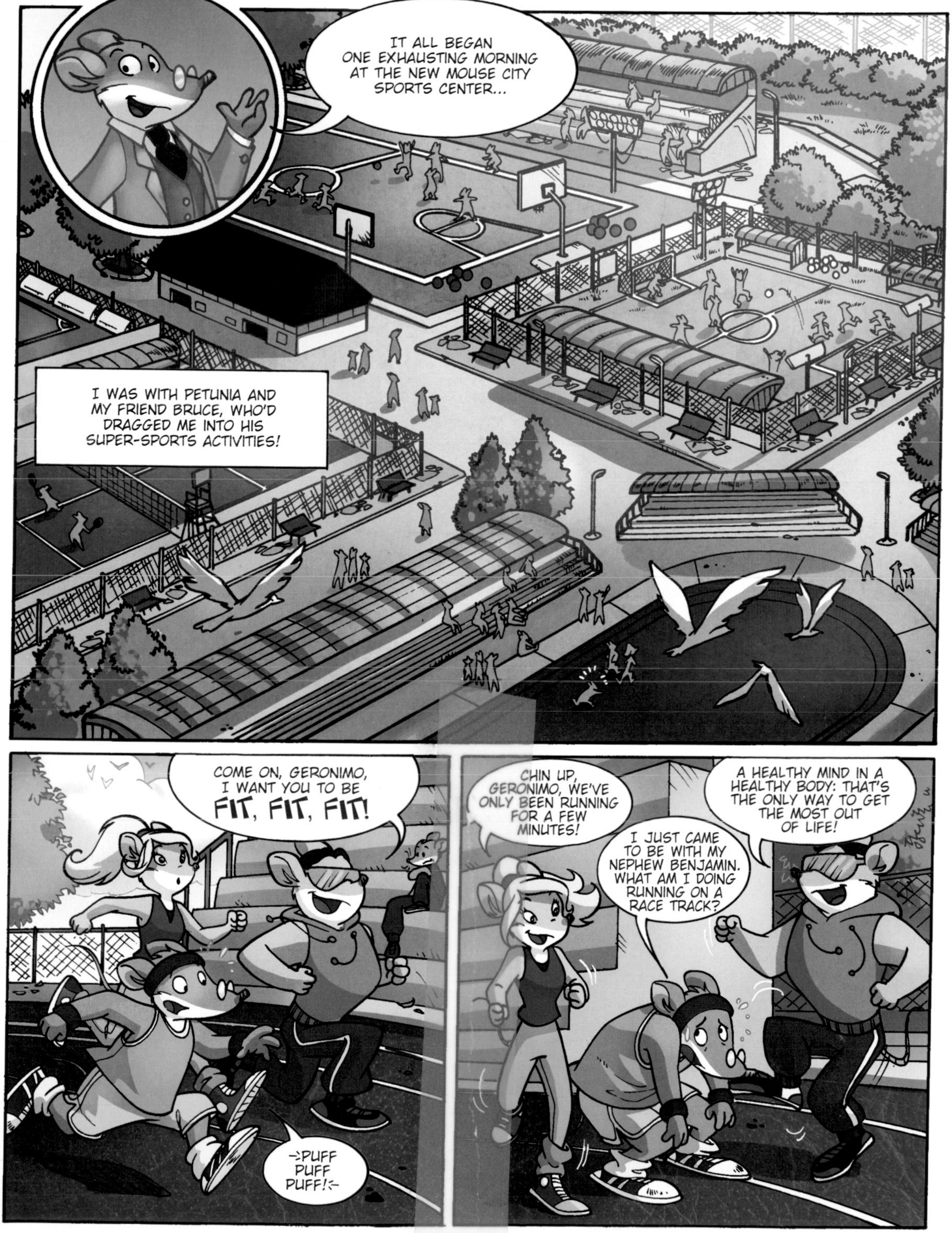
IT ALL BEGAN ONE EXHAUSTING MORNING AT THE NEW MOUSE CITY SPORTS CENTER...
I WAS WITH PETUNIA AND MY FRIEND BRUCE, WHO'D DRAGGED ME INTO HIS SUPER-SPORTS ACTIVITIES!
COME ON, GERONIMO, I WANT YOU TO BE FIT, FIT, FIT!
PUFF PUFF PUFF!
CHIN UP, GERONIMO, WE'VE ONLY BEEN RUNNING FOR A FEW MINUTES!
I JUST CAME TO BE WITH MY NEPHEW BENJAMIN. WHAT AM I DOING RUNNING ON A RACE TRACK?
A HEALTHY MIND IN A HEALTHY BODY: THAT'S THE ONLY WAY TO GET THE MOST OUT OF LIFE!

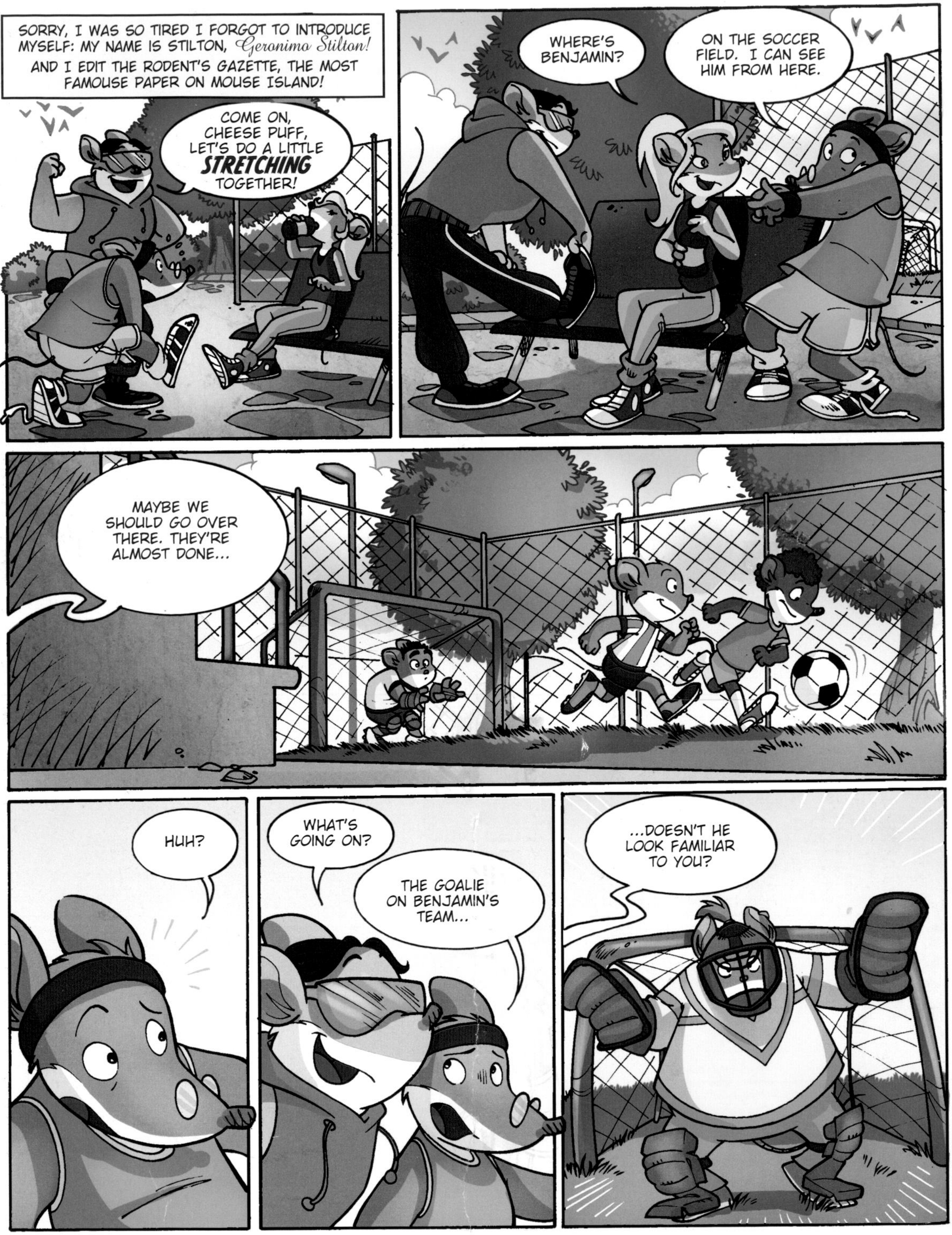
SORRY, I WAS SO TIRED I FORGOT TO INTRODUCE MYSELF: MY NAME IS STILTON, Geronimo Stilton! AND I EDIT THE RODENT'S GAZETTE, THE MOST FAMOUSE PAPER ON MOUSE ISLAND!
COME ON, CHEESE PUFF, LET'S DO A LITTLE STRETCHING TOGETHER!
WHERE'S BENJAMIN?
ON THE SOCCER FIELD. I CAN SEE HIM FROM HERE.
MAYBE WE SHOULD GO OVER THERE. THEY'RE ALMOST DONE...
HUH?
WHAT'S GOING ON?
THE GOALIE ON BENJAMIN'S TEAM...
...DOESN'T HE LOOK FAMILIAR TO YOU?

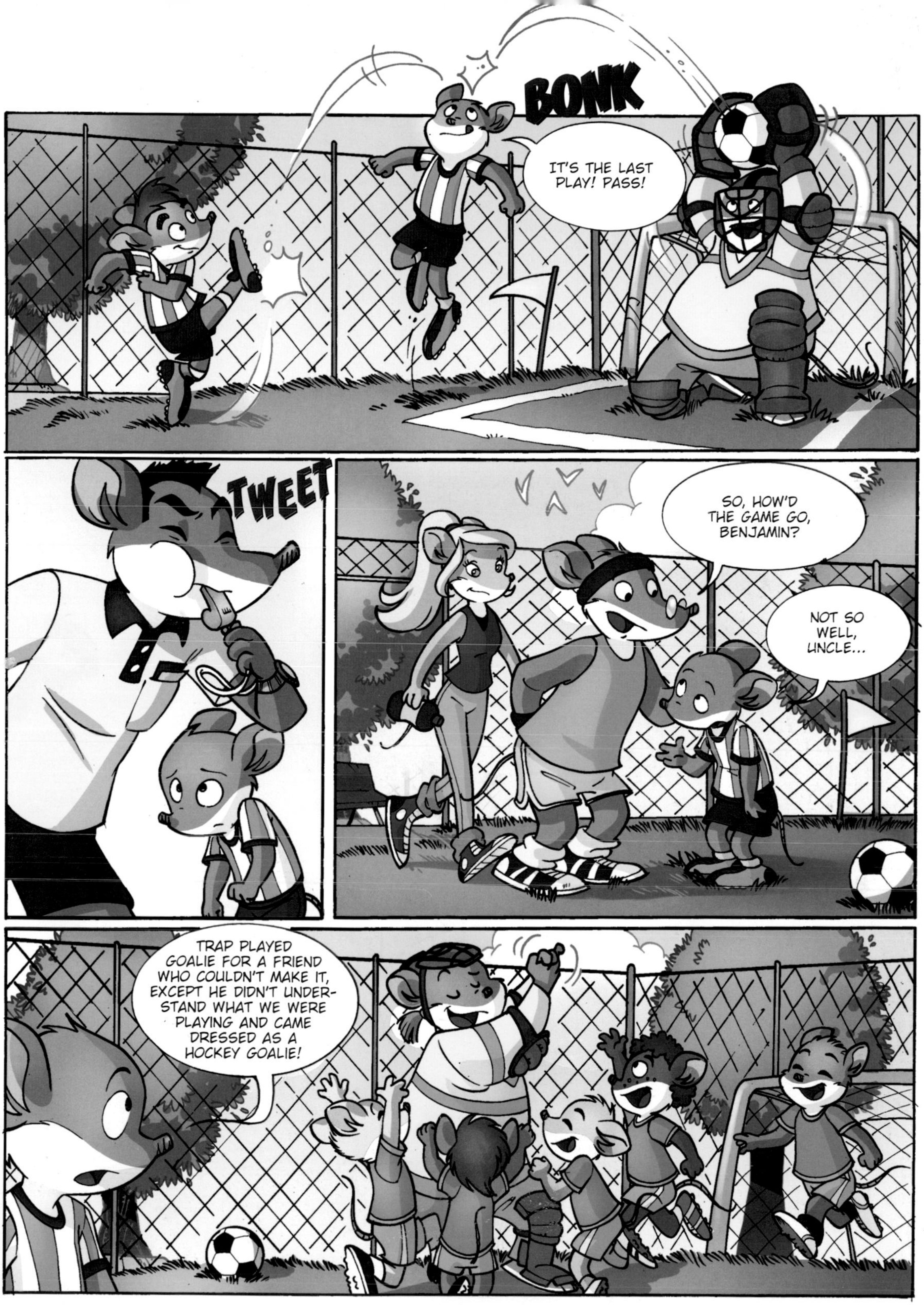
BONK
IT'S THE LAST PLAY! PASS!
TWEET
SO, HOW'D THE GAME GO, BENJAMIN?
NOT SO WELL, UNCLE...
TRAP PLAYED GOALIE FOR A FRIEND WHO COULDN'T MAKE IT, EXCEPT HE DIDN'T UNDER-STAND WHAT WE WERE PLAYING AND CAME DRESSED AS A HOCKEY GOALIE!

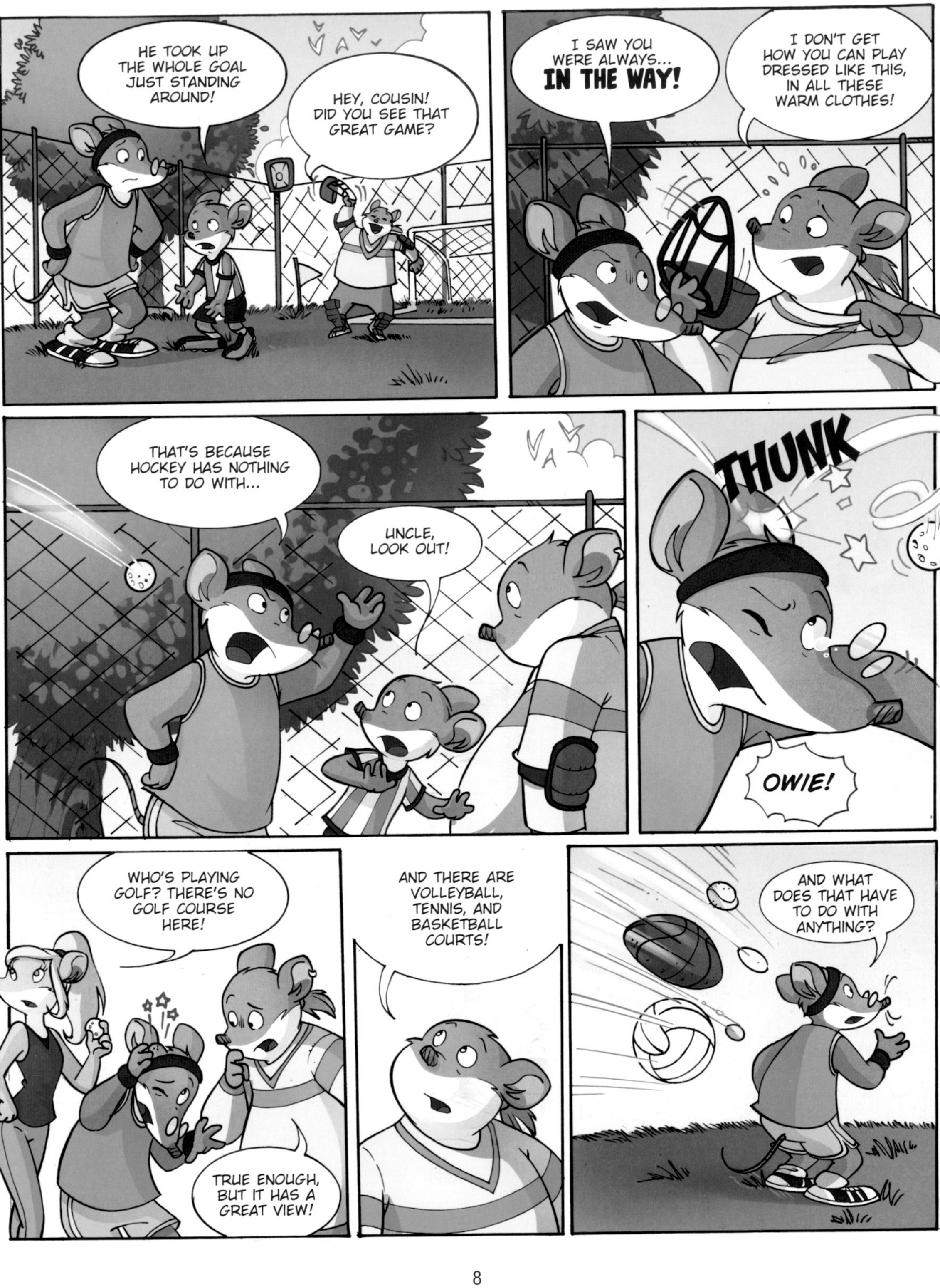
HE TOOK UP THE WHOLE GOAL JUST STANDING AROUND!
HEY, COUSIN! DID YOU SEE THAT GREAT GAME?
I SAW YOU WERE ALWAYS... IN THE WAY!
I DON'T GET HOW YOU CAN PLAY DRESSED LIKE THIS, IN ALL THESE WARM CLOTHES!
THAT'S BECAUSE HOCKEY HAS NOTHING TO DO WITH...
UNCLE, LOOK OUT!
THUNK
OWIE!
WHO'S PLAYING GOLF? THERE'S NO GOLF COURSE HERE!
TRUE ENOUGH, BUT IT HAS A GREAT VIEW!
AND THERE ARE VOLLEYBALL, TENNIS, AND BASKETBALL COURTS!
AND WHAT DOES THAT HAVE TO DO WITH ANYTHING?

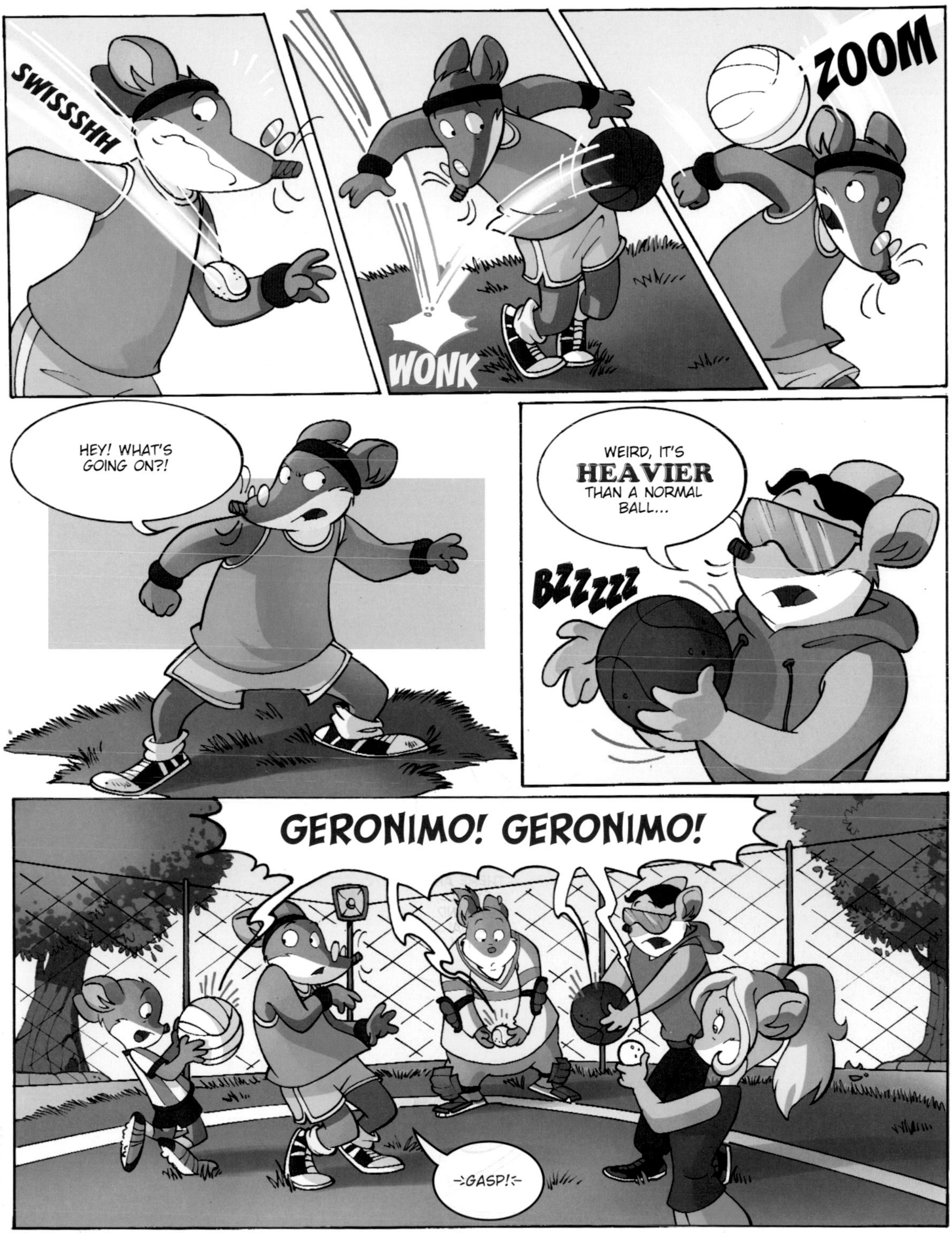
SWISSSHH
WONK
ZOOM
HEY! WHAT'S GOING ON?!
WEIRD, IT'S HEAVIER THAN A NORMAL BALL...
BZZZZZ
GERONIMO! GERONIMO!
GASP!

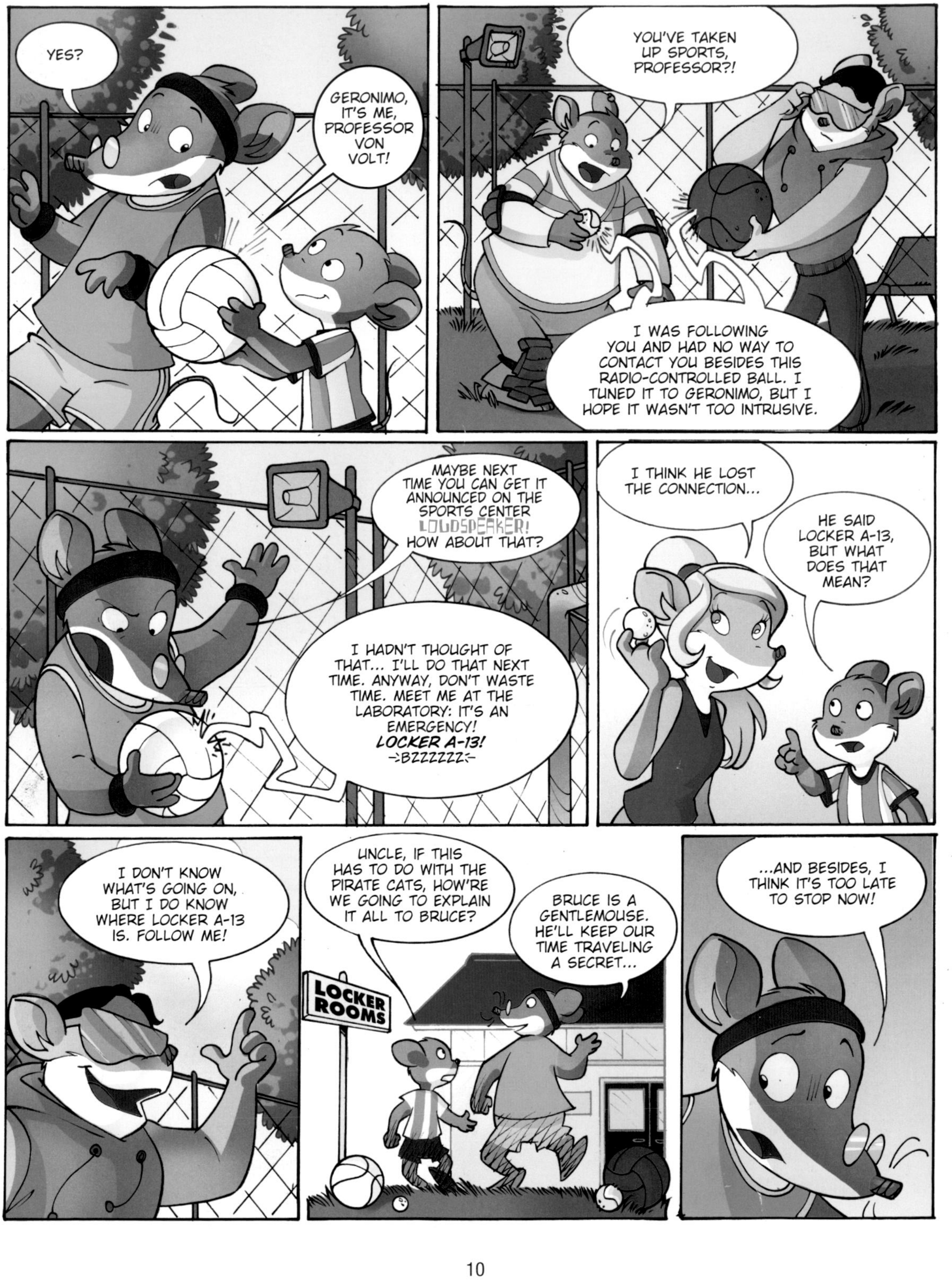
YES?
GERONIMO, IT'S ME, PROFESSOR VON VOLT!
YOU'VE TAKEN UP SPORTS, PROFESSOR?!
I WAS FOLLOWING YOU AND HAD NO WAY TO CONTACT YOU BESIDES THIS RADIO-CONTROLLED BALL. I TUNED IT TO GERONIMO, BUT I HOPE IT WASN'T TOO INTRUSIVE.
MAYBE NEXT TIME YOU CAN GET IT ANNOUNCED ON THE SPORTS CENTER LOUDSPEAKER! HOW ABOUT THAT?
I HADN'T THOUGHT OF THAT... I'LL DO THAT NEXT TIME. ANYWAY, DON'T WASTE TIME. MEET ME AT THE LABORATORY: IT'S AN EMERGENCY! LOCKER A-13! BZZZZZZ
I THINK HE LOST THE CONNECTION...
HE SAID LOCKER A-13, BUT WHAT DOES THAT MEAN?
I DON'T KNOW WHAT'S GOING ON, BUT I DO KNOW WHERE LOCKER A-13 IS. FOLLOW ME!
LOCKER ROOMS
UNCLE, IF THIS HAS TO DO WITH THE PIRATE CATS, HOW'RE WE GOING TO EXPLAIN IT ALL TO BRUCE?
BRUCE IS A GENTLEMOUSE. HE'LL KEEP OUR TIME TRAVELING A SECRET...
...AND BESIDES, I THINK IT'S TOO LATE TO STOP NOW!

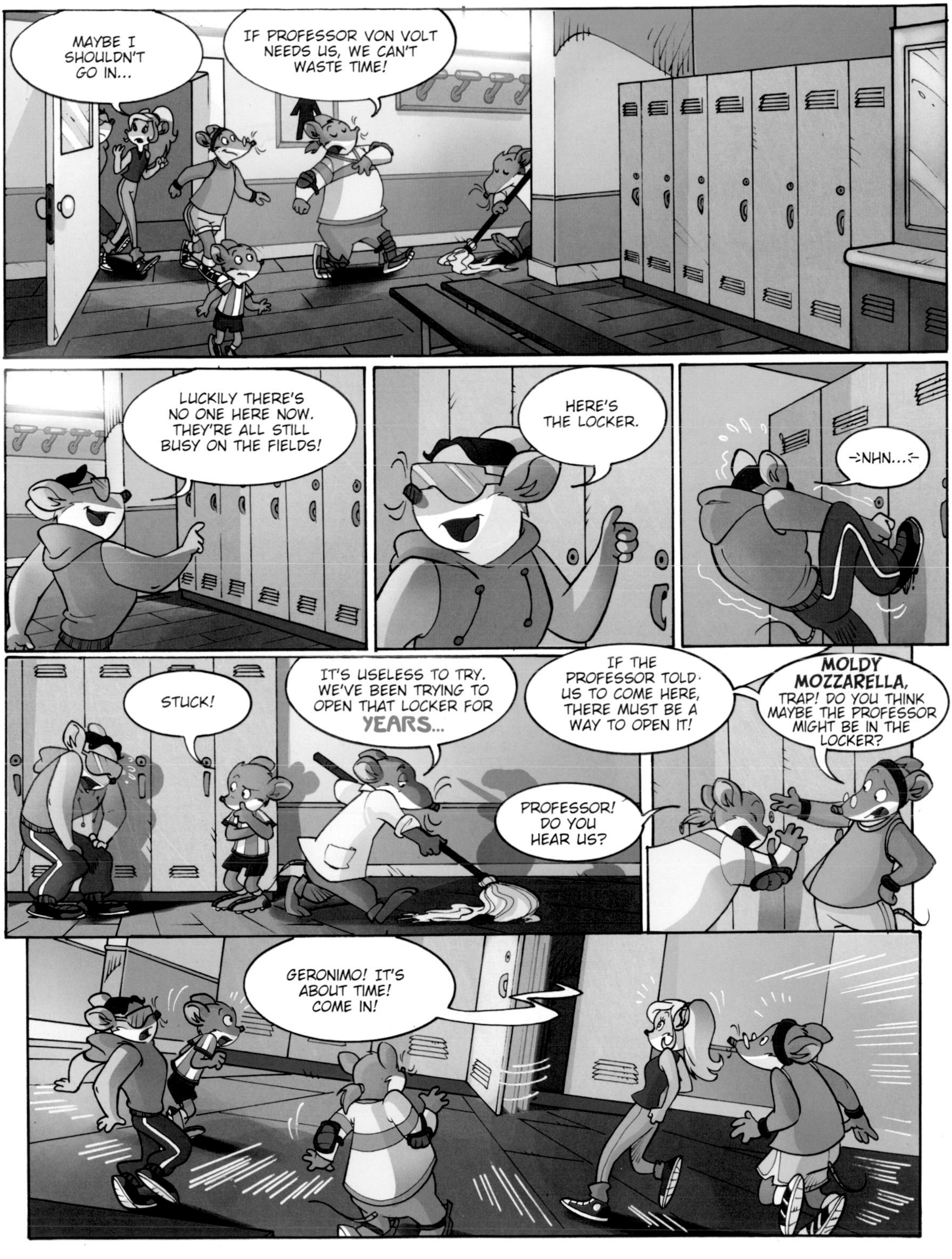

MAYBE I SHOULDN'T GO IN...
IF PROFESSOR VON VOLT NEEDS US, WE CAN'T WASTE TIME!
LUCKILY THERE'S NO ONE HERE NOW. THEY'RE ALL STILL BUSY ON THE FIELDS!
HERE'S THE LOCKER.
NHN...
STUCK!
IT'S USELESS TO TRY. WE'VE BEEN TRYING TO OPEN THAT LOCKER FOR YEARS...
IF THE PROFESSOR TOLD US TO COME HERE, THERE MUST BE A WAY TO OPEN IT!
PROFESSOR! DO YOU HEAR US?
MOLDY MOZZARELLA, TRAP! DO YOU THINK MAYBE THE PROFESSOR MIGHT BE IN THE LOCKER?
GERONIMO! IT'S ABOUT TIME! COME IN!

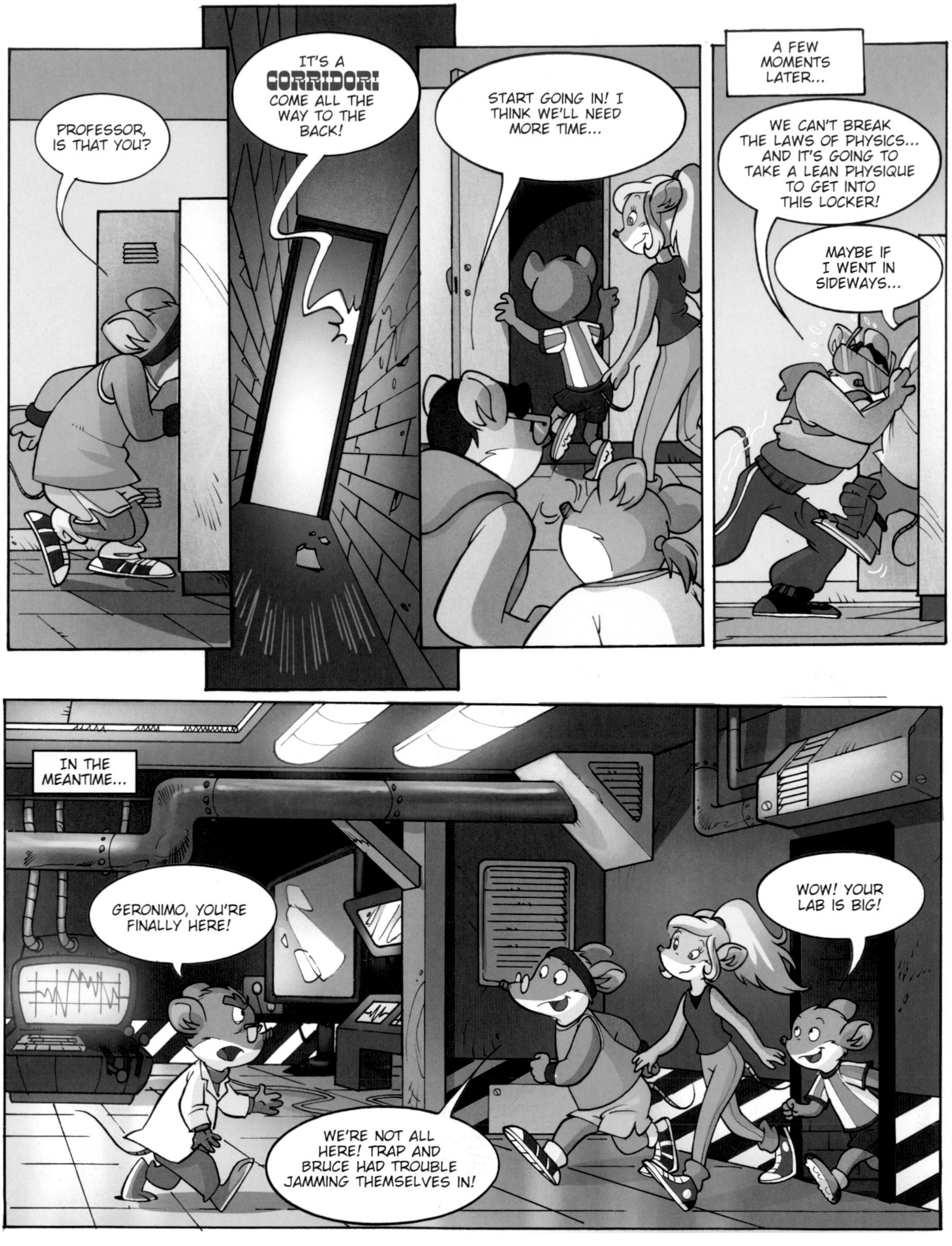
PROFESSOR, IS THAT YOU?
IT'S A CORRIDOR! COME ALL THE WAY TO THE BACK!
START GOING IN! I THINK WE'LL NEED MORE TIME...
A FEW MOMENTS LATER...
WE CAN'T BREAK THE LAWS OF PHYSICS... AND IT'S GOING TO TAKE A LEAN PHYSIQUE TO GET INTO THIS LOCKER!
MAYBE IF I WENT IN SIDEWAYS...
IN THE MEANTIME...
GERONIMO, YOU'RE FINALLY HERE!
WOW! YOUR LAB IS BIG!
WE'RE NOT ALL HERE! TRAP AND BRUCE HAD TROUBLE JAMMING THEMSELVES IN!

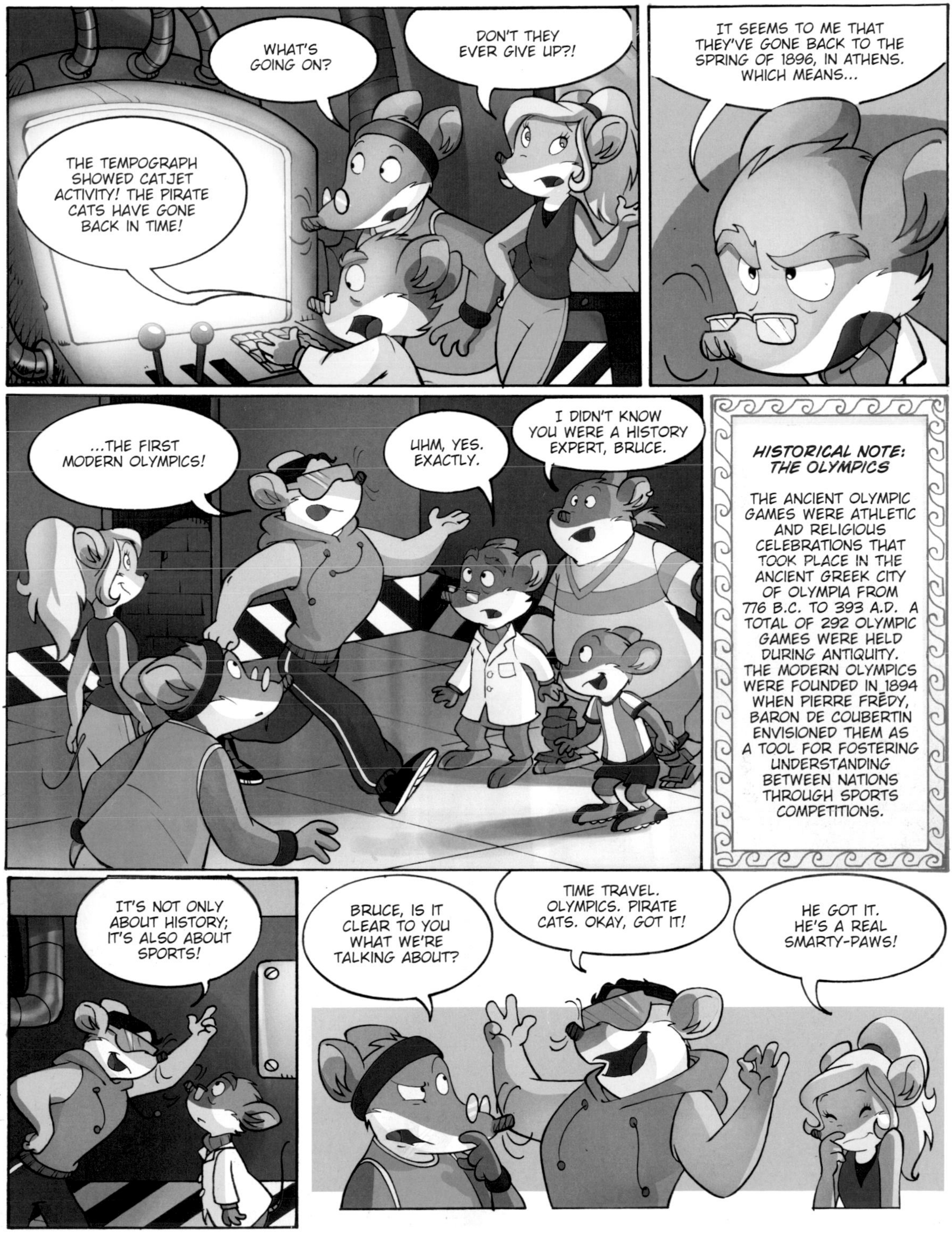
WHAT'S GOING ON?
DON'T THEY EVER GIVE UP?!
THE TEMPOGRAPH SHOWED CATJET ACTIVITY! THE PIRATE CATS HAVE GONE BACK IN TIME!
IT SEEMS TO ME THAT THEY'VE GONE BACK TO THE SPRING OF 1896, IN ATHENS. WHICH MEANS...
...THE FIRST MODERN OLYMPICS!
UHM, YES. EXACTLY.
I DIDN'T KNOW YOU WERE A HISTORY EXPERT, BRUCE.
HISTORICAL NOTE: THE OLYMPICS
THE ANCIENT OLYMPIC GAMES WERE ATHLETIC AND RELIGIOUS CELEBRATIONS THAT TOOK PLACE IN THE ANCIENT GREEK CITY OF OLYMPIA FROM 776 B.C. TO 393 A.D. A TOTAL OF 292 OLYMPIC GAMES WERE HELD DURING ANTIQUITY. THE MODERN OLYMPICS WERE FOUNDED IN 1894 WHEN PIERRE FRÉDY, BARON DE COUBERTIN ENVISIONED THEM AS A TOOL FOR FOSTERING UNDERSTANDING BETWEEN NATIONS THROUGH SPORTS COMPETITIONS.
IT'S NOT ONLY ABOUT HISTORY; IT'S ALSO ABOUT SPORTS!
BRUCE, IS IT CLEAR TO YOU WHAT WE'RE TALKING ABOUT?
TIME TRAVEL. OLYMPICS. PIRATE CATS. OKAY, GOT IT!
HE GOT IT. HE'S A REAL SMARTY-PAWS!

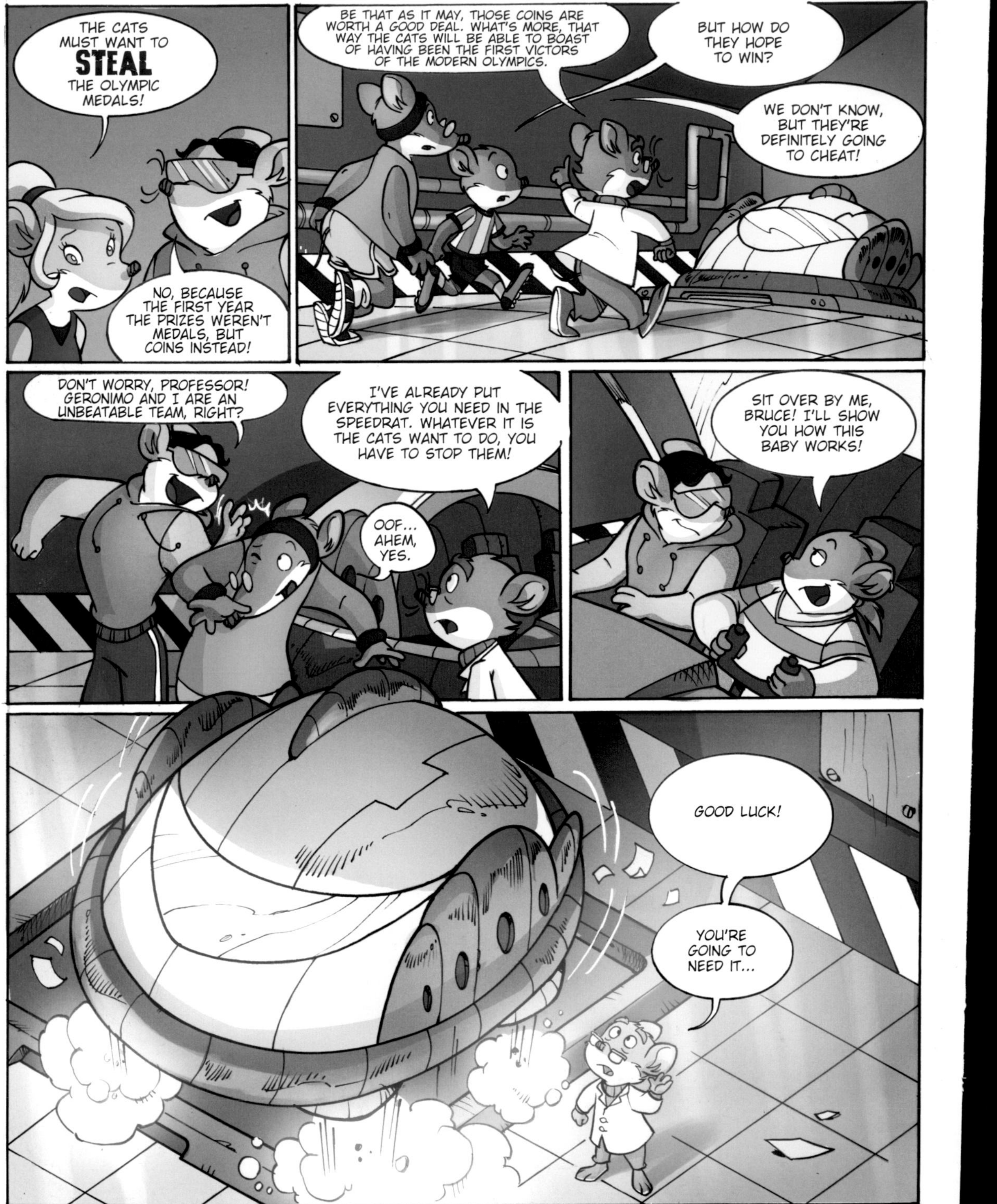
THE CATS MUST WANT TO STEAL THE OLYMPIC MEDALS!
NO, BECAUSE THE FIRST YEAR THE PRIZES WEREN'T MEDALS, BUT COINS INSTEAD!
BE THAT AS IT MAY, THOSE COINS ARE WORTH A GOOD DEAL. WHAT'S MORE, THAT WAY THE CATS WILL BE ABLE TO BOAST OF HAVING BEEN THE FIRST VICTORS OF THE MODERN OLYMPICS.
BUT HOW DO THEY HOPE TO WIN?
WE DON'T KNOW, BUT THEY'RE DEFINITELY GOING TO CHEAT!
DON'T WORRY, PROFESSOR! GERONIMO AND I ARE AN UNBEATABLE TEAM, RIGHT?
I'VE ALREADY PUT EVERYTHING YOU NEED IN THE SPEEDRAT. WHATEVER IT IS THE CATS WANT TO DO, YOU HAVE TO STOP THEM!
OOF... AHEM, YES.
SIT OVER BY ME, BRUCE! I'LL SHOW YOU HOW THIS BABY WORKS!
GOOD LUCK!
YOU'RE GOING TO NEED IT...

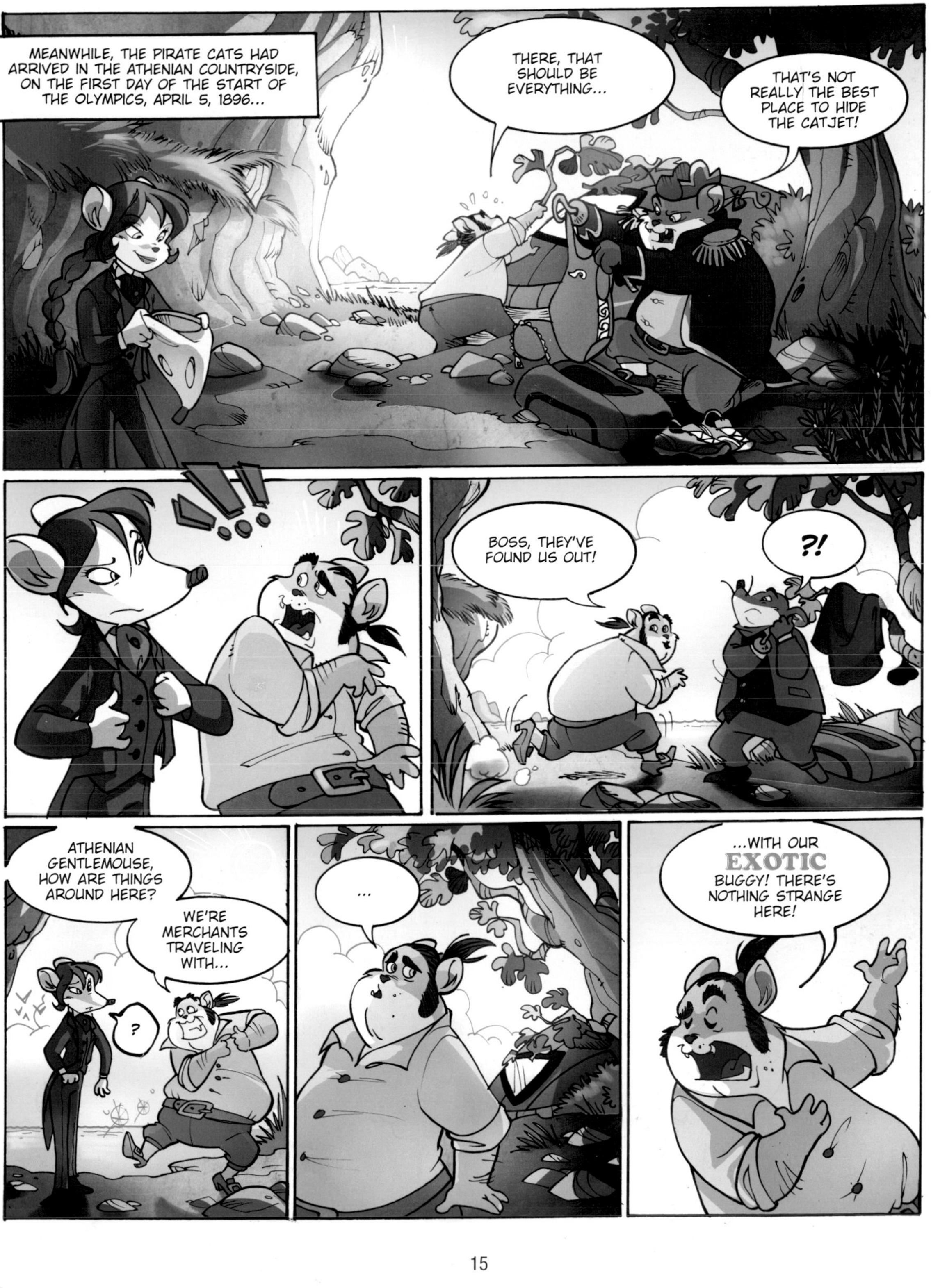

MEANWHILE, THE PIRATE CATS HAD ARRIVED IN THE ATHENIAN COUNTRYSIDE, ON THE FIRST DAY OF THE START OF THE OLYMPICS, APRIL 5, 1896...
THERE, THAT SHOULD BE EVERYTHING...
THAT'S NOT REALLY THE BEST PLACE TO HIDE THE CATJET!
BOSS, THEY'VE FOUND US OUT!
?!
ATHENIAN GENTLEMOUSE, HOW ARE THINGS AROUND HERE?
WE'RE MERCHANTS TRAVELING WITH...
?
...
...WITH OUR EXOTIC BUGGY! THERE'S NOTHING STRANGE HERE!

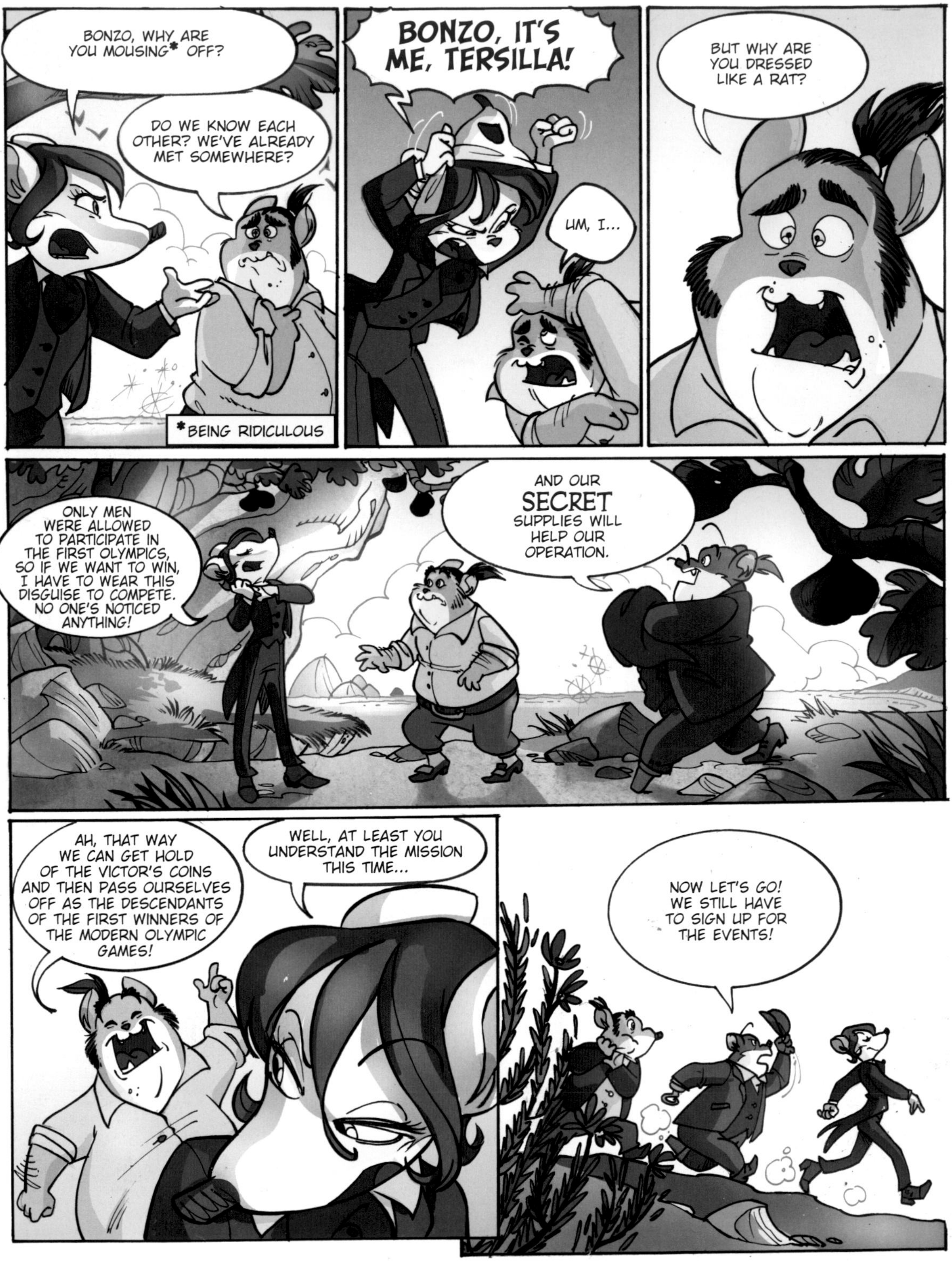
BONZO, WHY ARE YOU MOUSING* OFF?
DO WE KNOW EACH OTHER? WE'VE ALREADY MET SOMEWHERE?
*BEING RIDICULOUS
BONZO, IT'S ME, TERSILLA!
UM, I...
BUT WHY ARE YOU DRESSED LIKE A RAT?
ONLY MEN WERE ALLOWED TO PARTICIPATE IN THE FIRST OLYMPICS, SO IF WE WANT TO WIN, I HAVE TO WEAR THIS DISGUISE TO COMPETE. NO ONE'S NOTICED ANYTHING!
AND OUR SECRET SUPPLIES WILL HELP OUR OPERATION.
AH, THAT WAY WE CAN GET HOLD OF THE VICTOR'S COINS AND THEN PASS OURSELVES OFF AS THE DESCENDANTS OF THE FIRST WINNERS OF THE MODERN OLYMPIC GAMES!
WELL, AT LEAST YOU UNDERSTAND THE MISSION THIS TIME...
NOW LET'S GO! WE STILL HAVE TO SIGN UP FOR THE EVENTS!

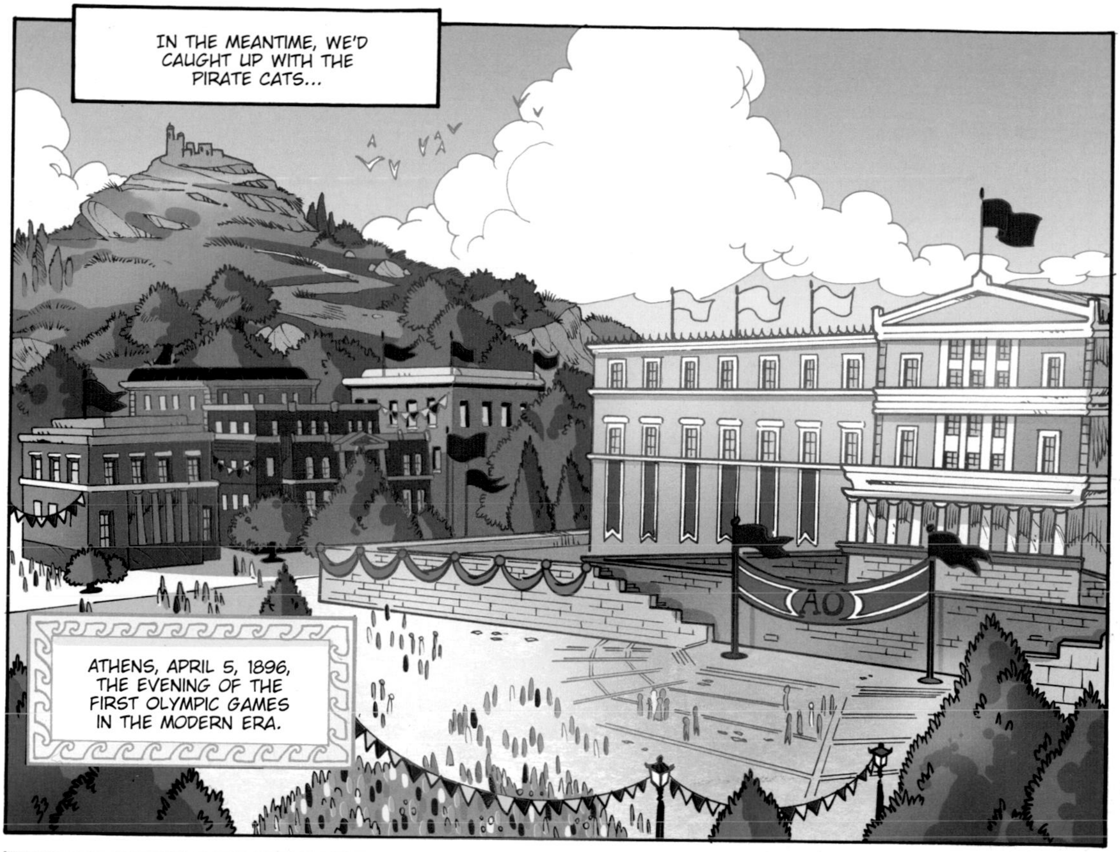
IN THE MEANTIME, WE'D CAUGHT UP WITH THE PIRATE CATS...
ATHENS, APRIL 5, 1896, THE EVENING OF THE FIRST OLYMPIC GAMES IN THE MODERN ERA.

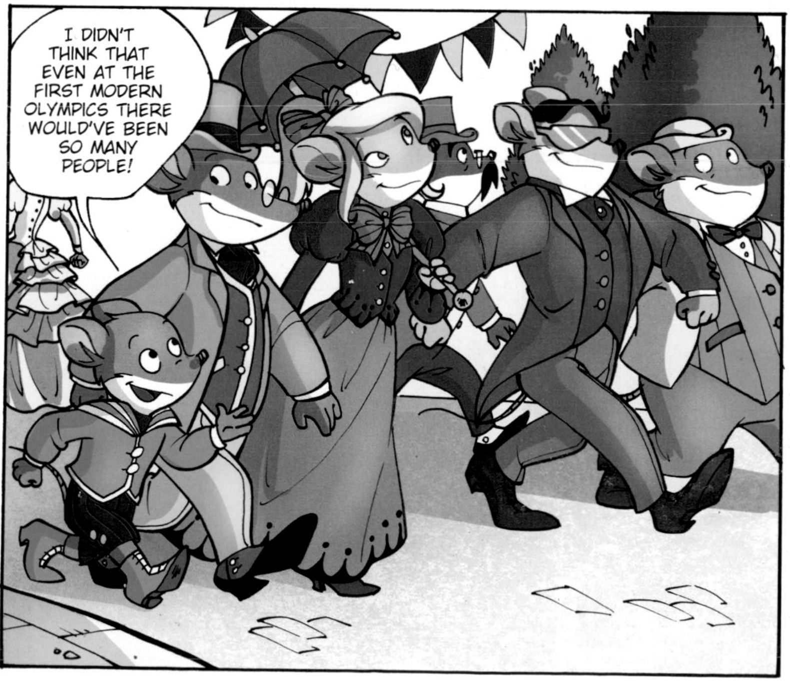
I DIDN'T THINK THAT EVEN AT THE FIRST MODERN OLYMPICS THERE WOULD'VE BEEN SO MANY PEOPLE!

HISTORICAL NOTE: THE MODERN OLYMPICS

THE OLYMPIC GAMES ARE HELD EVERY FOUR YEARS AND ARE A COMPETITION BETWEEN THE BEST ATHLETES IN THE WORLD IN NEARLY ALL THE SPORTS PLAYED ON THE FIVE CONTINENTS. THE NAME OLYMPICS WAS CHOSEN TO COMMEMORATE THE GAMES THAT TOOK PLACE IN ANCIENT GREECE NEAR THE CITY OF OLYMPIA, WHEN THE BEST GREEK ATHLETES COMPETED AGAINST EACH OTHER.

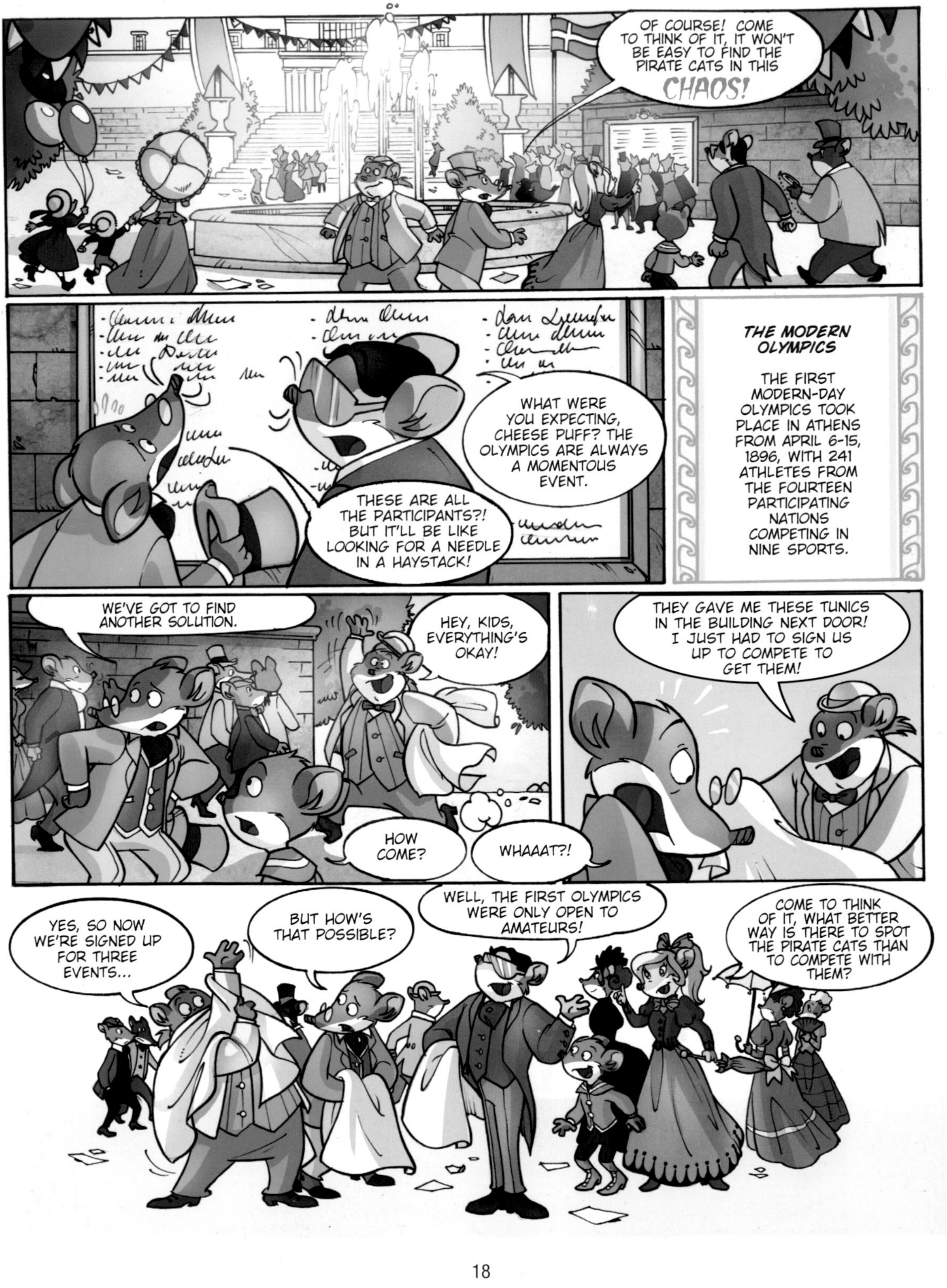
OF COURSE! COME TO THINK OF IT, IT WON'T BE EASY TO FIND THE PIRATE CATS IN THIS CHAOS!
THESE ARE ALL THE PARTICIPANTS?! BUT IT'LL BE LIKE LOOKING FOR A NEEDLE IN A HAYSTACK!
WHAT WERE YOU EXPECTING, CHEESE PUFF? THE OLYMPICS ARE ALWAYS A MOMENTOUS EVENT.
THE MODERN OLYMPICS
THE FIRST MODERN-DAY OLYMPICS TOOK PLACE IN ATHENS FROM APRIL 6-15, 1896, WITH 241 ATHLETES FROM THE FOURTEEN PARTICIPATING NATIONS COMPETING IN NINE SPORTS.
WE'VE GOT TO FIND ANOTHER SOLUTION.
HEY, KIDS, EVERYTHING'S OKAY!
HOW COME?
THEY GAVE ME THESE TUNICS IN THE BUILDING NEXT DOOR! I JUST HAD TO SIGN US UP TO COMPETE TO GET THEM!
WHAAAT?!
YES, SO NOW WE'RE SIGNED UP FOR THREE EVENTS...
BUT HOW'S THAT POSSIBLE?
WELL, THE FIRST OLYMPICS WERE ONLY OPEN TO AMATEURS!
COME TO THINK OF IT, WHAT BETTER WAY IS THERE TO SPOT THE PIRATE CATS THAN TO COMPETE WITH THEM?

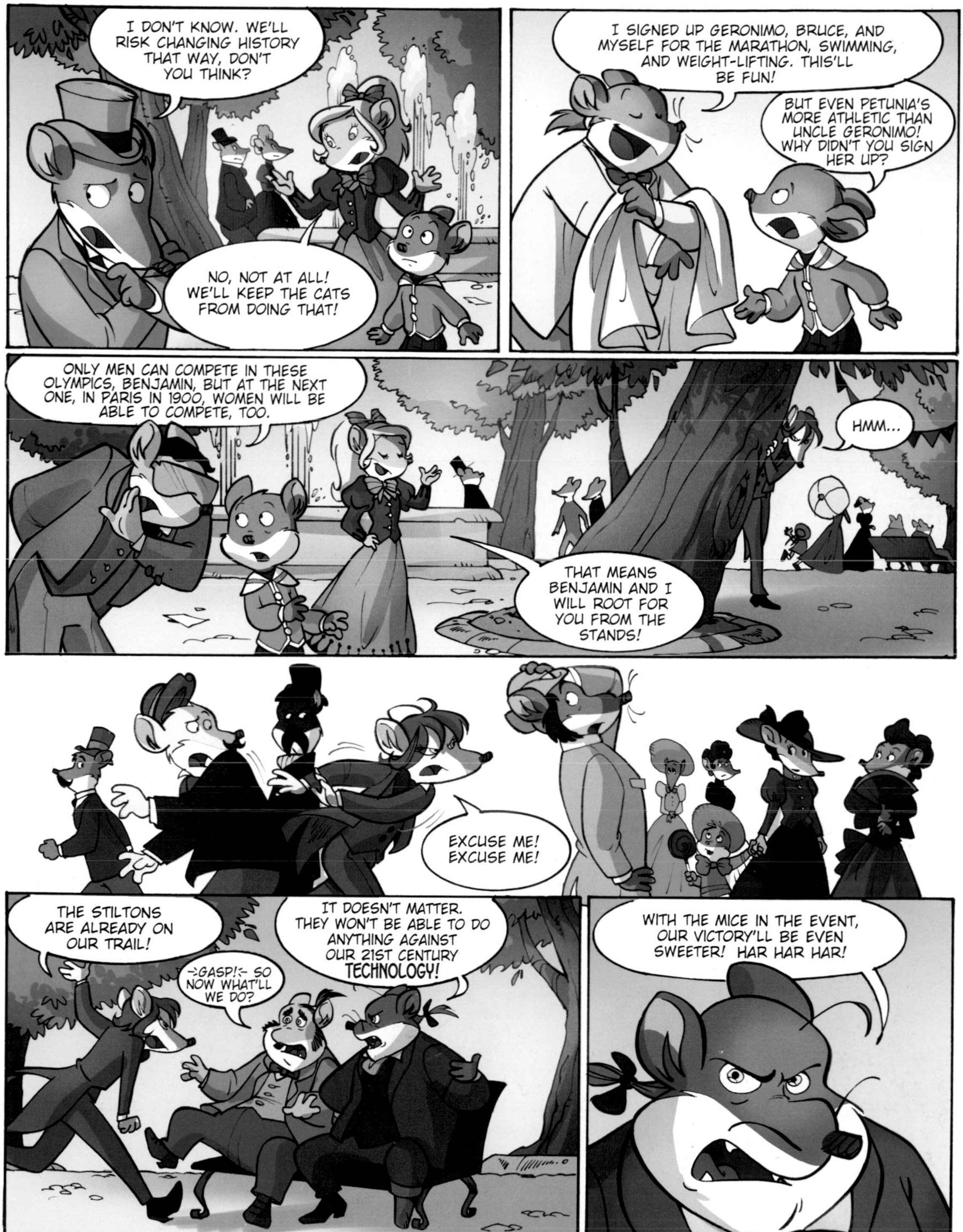
I DON'T KNOW. WE'LL RISK CHANGING HISTORY THAT WAY, DON'T YOU THINK?
NO, NOT AT ALL! WE'LL KEEP THE CATS FROM DOING THAT!
I SIGNED UP GERONIMO, BRUCE, AND MYSELF FOR THE MARATHON, SWIMMING, AND WEIGHT-LIFTING. THIS'LL BE FUN!
BUT EVEN PETUNIA'S MORE ATHLETIC THAN UNCLE GERONIMO! WHY DIDN'T YOU SIGN HER UP?
ONLY MEN CAN COMPETE IN THESE OLYMPICS, BENJAMIN, BUT AT THE NEXT ONE, IN PARIS IN 1900, WOMEN WILL BE ABLE TO COMPETE, TOO.
THAT MEANS BENJAMIN AND I WILL ROOT FOR YOU FROM THE STANDS!
HMM...
EXCUSE ME! EXCUSE ME!
THE STILTONS ARE ALREADY ON OUR TRAIL!
-GASP!- SO NOW WHAT'LL WE DO?
IT DOESN'T MATTER. THEY WON'T BE ABLE TO DO ANYTHING AGAINST OUR 21ST CENTURY TECHNOLOGY!
WITH THE MICE IN THE EVENT, OUR VICTORY'LL BE EVEN SWEETER! HAR HAR HAR!

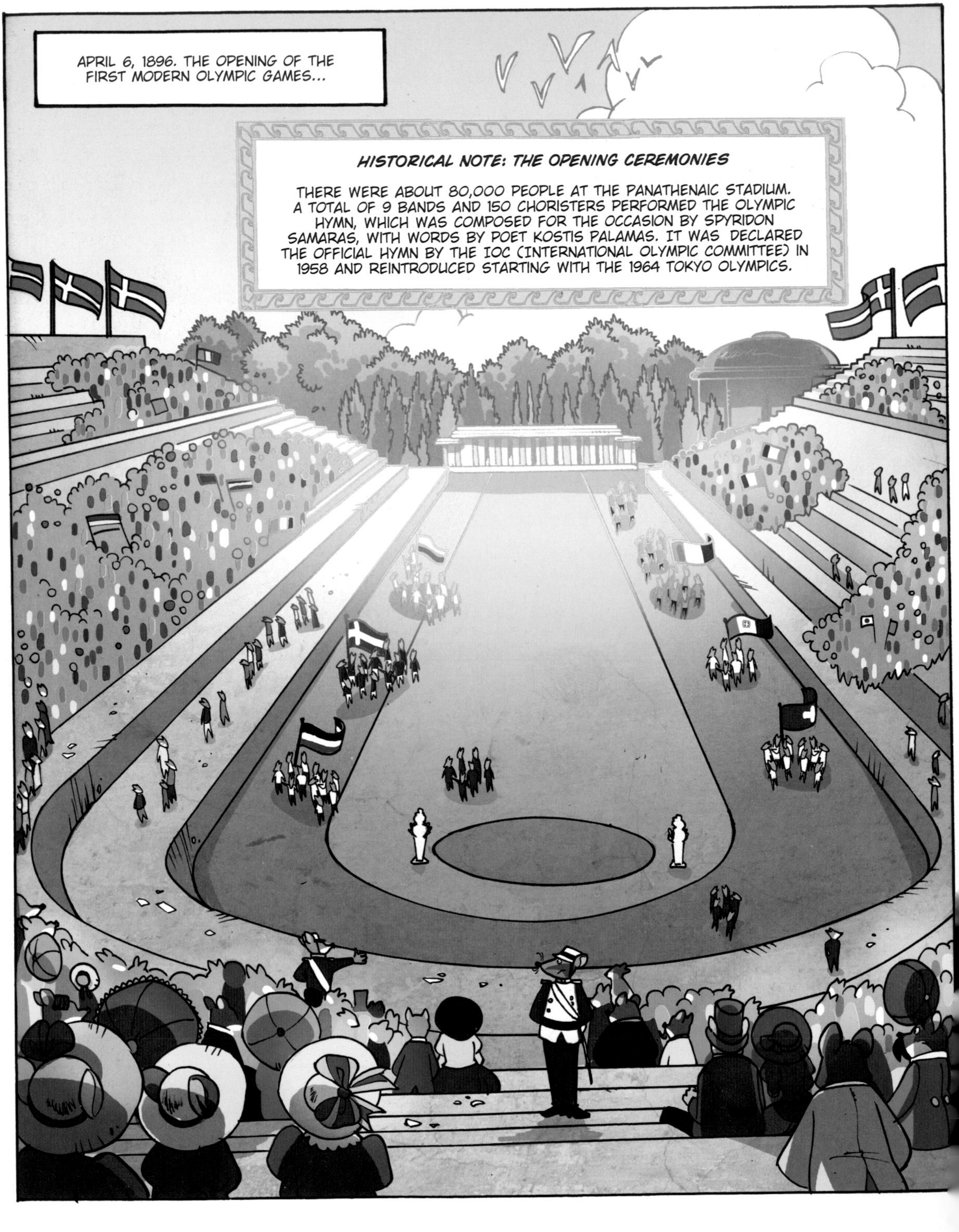
APRIL 6, 1896. THE OPENING OF THE FIRST MODERN OLYMPIC GAMES...
HISTORICAL NOTE: THE OPENING CEREMONIES
THERE WERE ABOUT 80,000 PEOPLE AT THE PANATHENAIC STADIUM. A TOTAL OF 9 BANDS AND 150 CHORISTERS PERFORMED THE OLYMPIC HYMN, WHICH WAS COMPOSED FOR THE OCCASION BY SPYRIDON SAMARAS, WITH WORDS BY POET KOSTIS PALAMAS. IT WAS DECLARED THE OFFICIAL HYMN BY THE IOC (INTERNATIONAL OLYMPIC COMMITTEE) IN 1958 AND REINTRODUCED STARTING WITH THE 1964 TOKYO OLYMPICS.

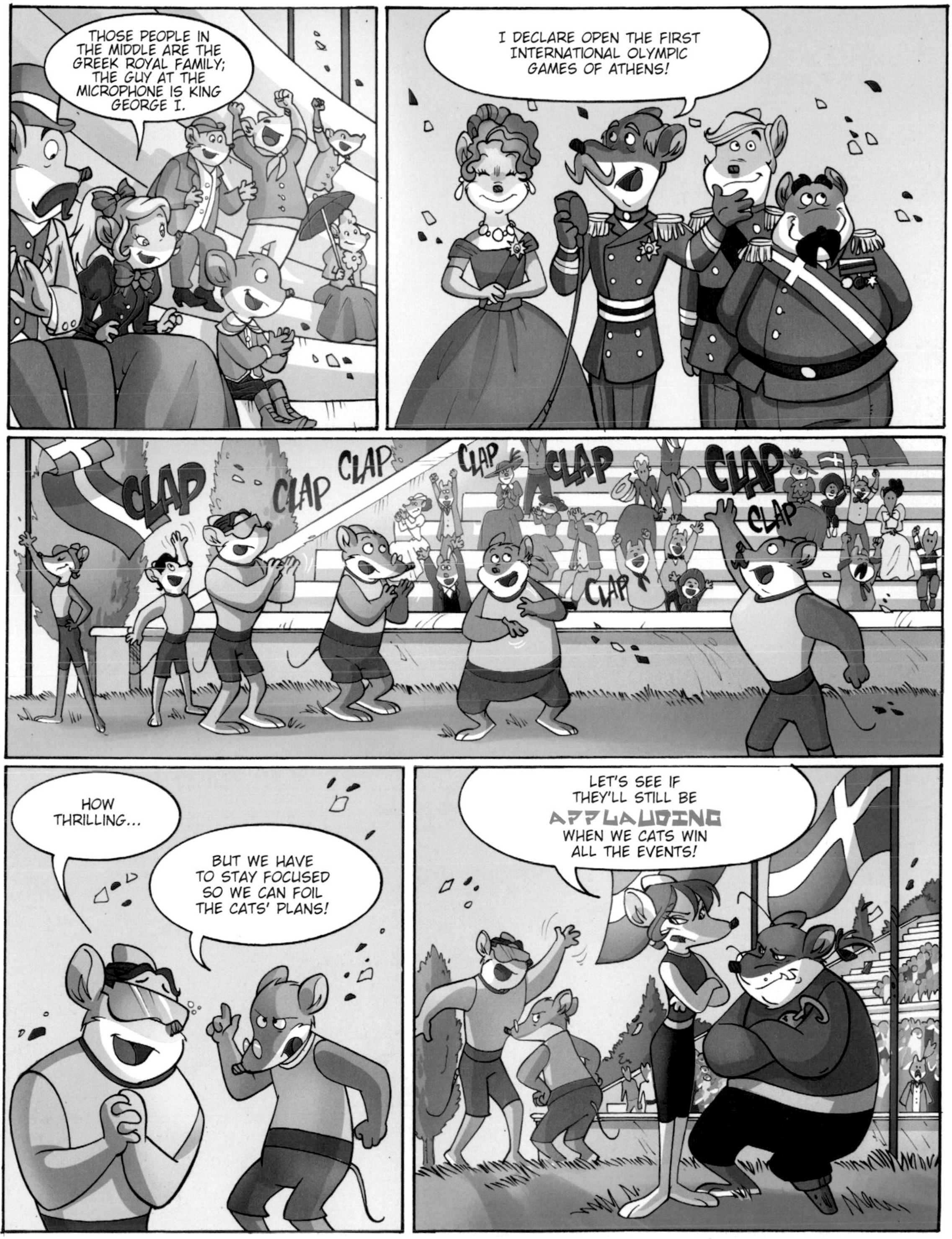
THOSE PEOPLE IN THE MIDDLE ARE THE GREEK ROYAL FAMILY; THE GUY AT THE MICROPHONE IS KING GEORGE I.
I DECLARE OPEN THE FIRST INTERNATIONAL OLYMPIC GAMES OF ATHENS!
CLAP
CLAP
CLAP
CLAP
CLAP
CLAP
CLAP
CLAP
HOW THRILLING...
BUT WE HAVE TO STAY FOCUSED SO WE CAN FOIL THE CATS' PLANS!
LET'S SEE IF THEY'LL STILL BE APPLAUDING WHEN WE CATS WIN ALL THE EVENTS!

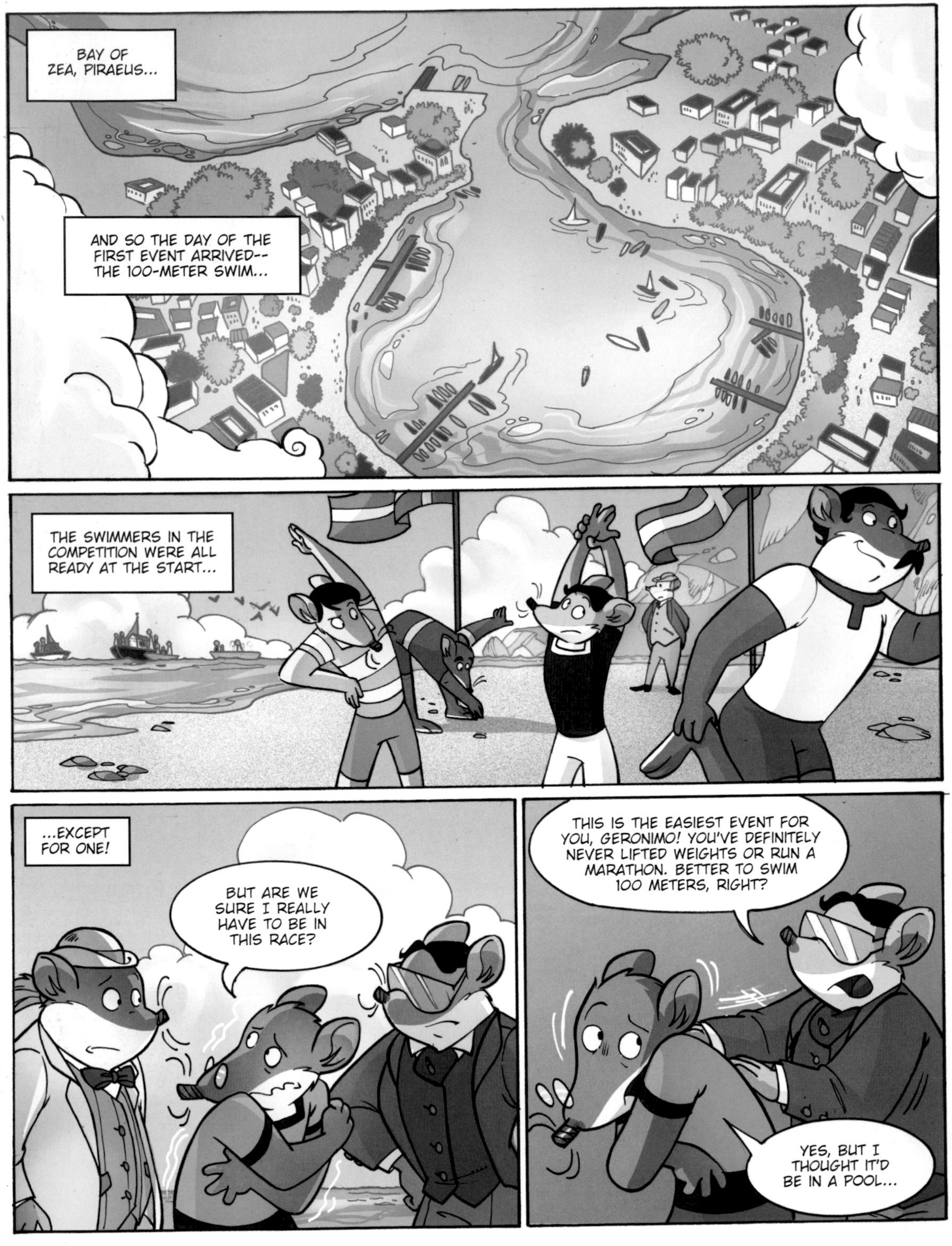
BAY OF ZEA, PIRAEUS...
AND SO THE DAY OF THE FIRST EVENT ARRIVED-- THE 100-METER SWIM...
THE SWIMMERS IN THE COMPETITION WERE ALL READY AT THE START...
...EXCEPT FOR ONE!
BUT ARE WE SURE I REALLY HAVE TO BE IN THIS RACE?
THIS IS THE EASIEST EVENT FOR YOU, GERONIMO! YOU'VE DEFINITELY NEVER LIFTED WEIGHTS OR RUN A MARATHON. BETTER TO SWIM 100 METERS, RIGHT?
YES, BUT I THOUGHT IT'D BE IN A POOL...

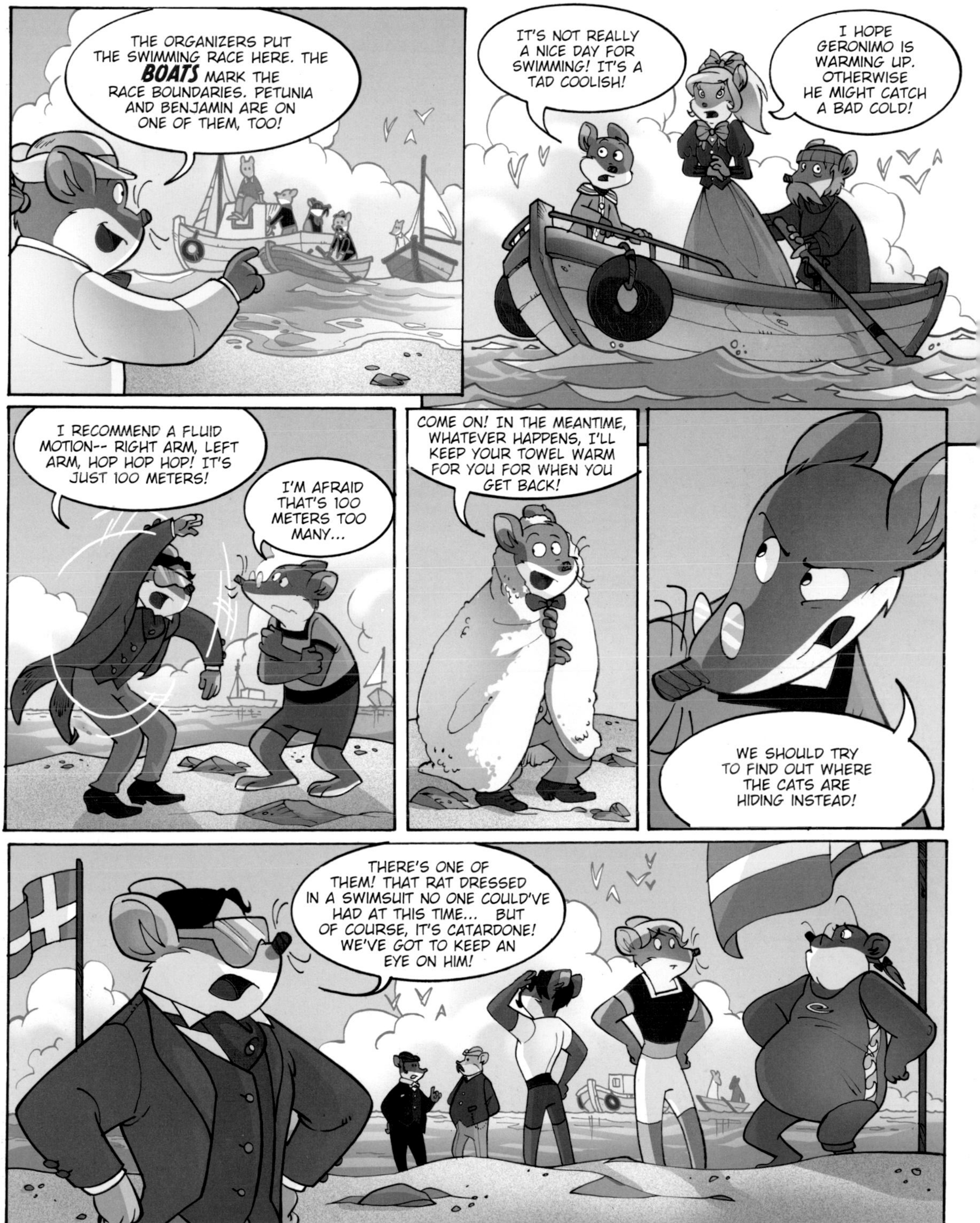

THE ORGANIZERS PUT THE SWIMMING RACE HERE. THE BOATS MARK THE RACE BOUNDARIES. PETUNIA AND BENJAMIN ARE ON ONE OF THEM, TOO!
IT'S NOT REALLY A NICE DAY FOR SWIMMING! IT'S A TAD COOLISH!
I HOPE GERONIMO IS WARMING UP. OTHERWISE HE MIGHT CATCH A BAD COLD!
I RECOMMEND A FLUID MOTION-- RIGHT ARM, LEFT ARM, HOP HOP HOP! IT'S JUST 100 METERS!
I'M AFRAID THAT'S 100 METERS TOO MANY...
COME ON! IN THE MEANTIME, WHATEVER HAPPENS, I'LL KEEP YOUR TOWEL WARM FOR YOU FOR WHEN YOU GET BACK!
WE SHOULD TRY TO FIND OUT WHERE THE CATS ARE HIDING INSTEAD!
THERE'S ONE OF THEM! THAT RAT DRESSED IN A SWIMSUIT NO ONE COULD'VE HAD AT THIS TIME... BUT OF COURSE, IT'S CATARDONE! WE'VE GOT TO KEEP AN EYE ON HIM!

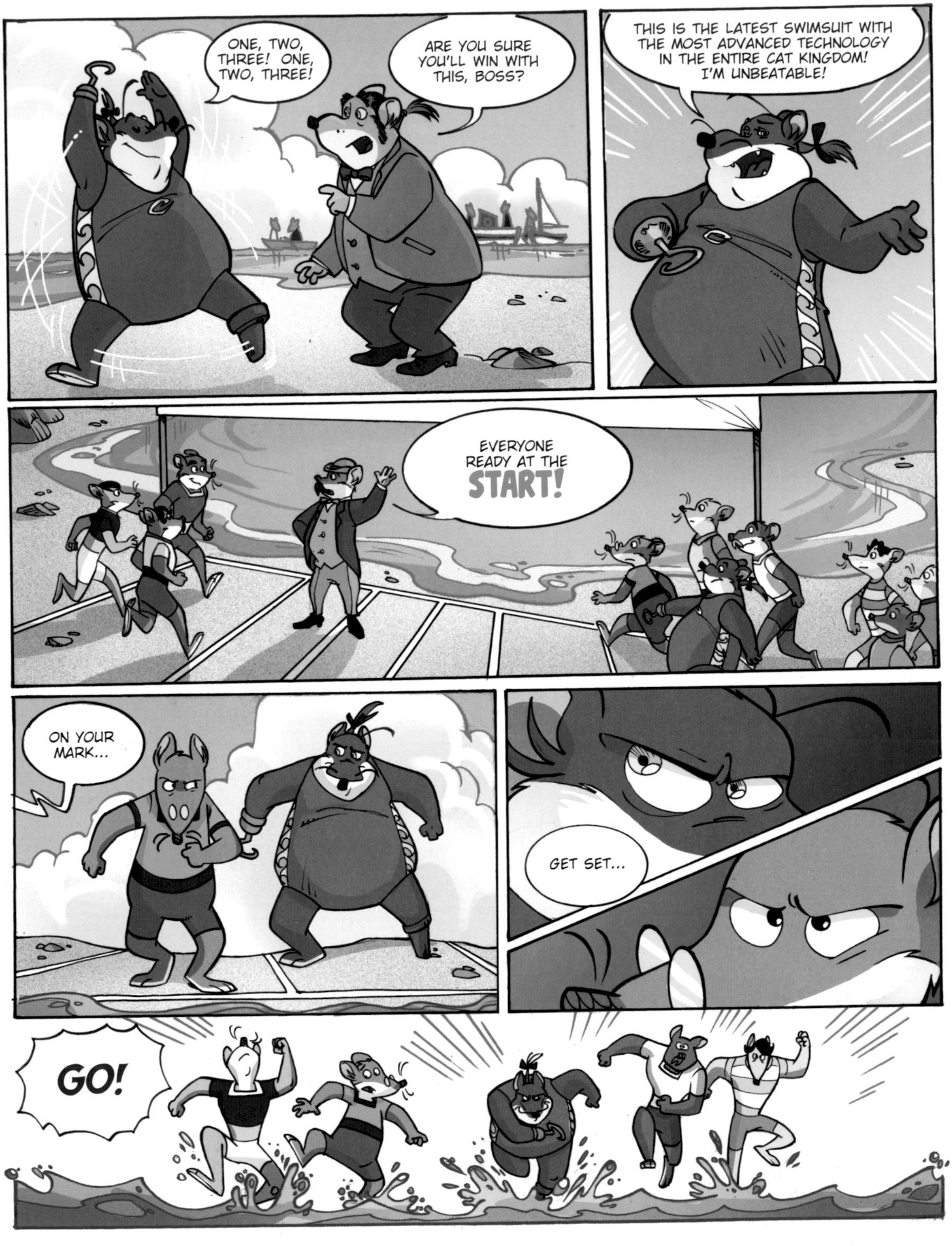
ONE, TWO, THREE! ONE, TWO, THREE!
ARE YOU SURE YOU'LL WIN WITH THIS, BOSS?
THIS IS THE LATEST SWIMSUIT WITH THE MOST ADVANCED TECHNOLOGY IN THE ENTIRE CAT KINGDOM! I'M UNBEATABLE!
EVERYONE READY AT THE START!
ON YOUR MARK...
GET SET...
GO!

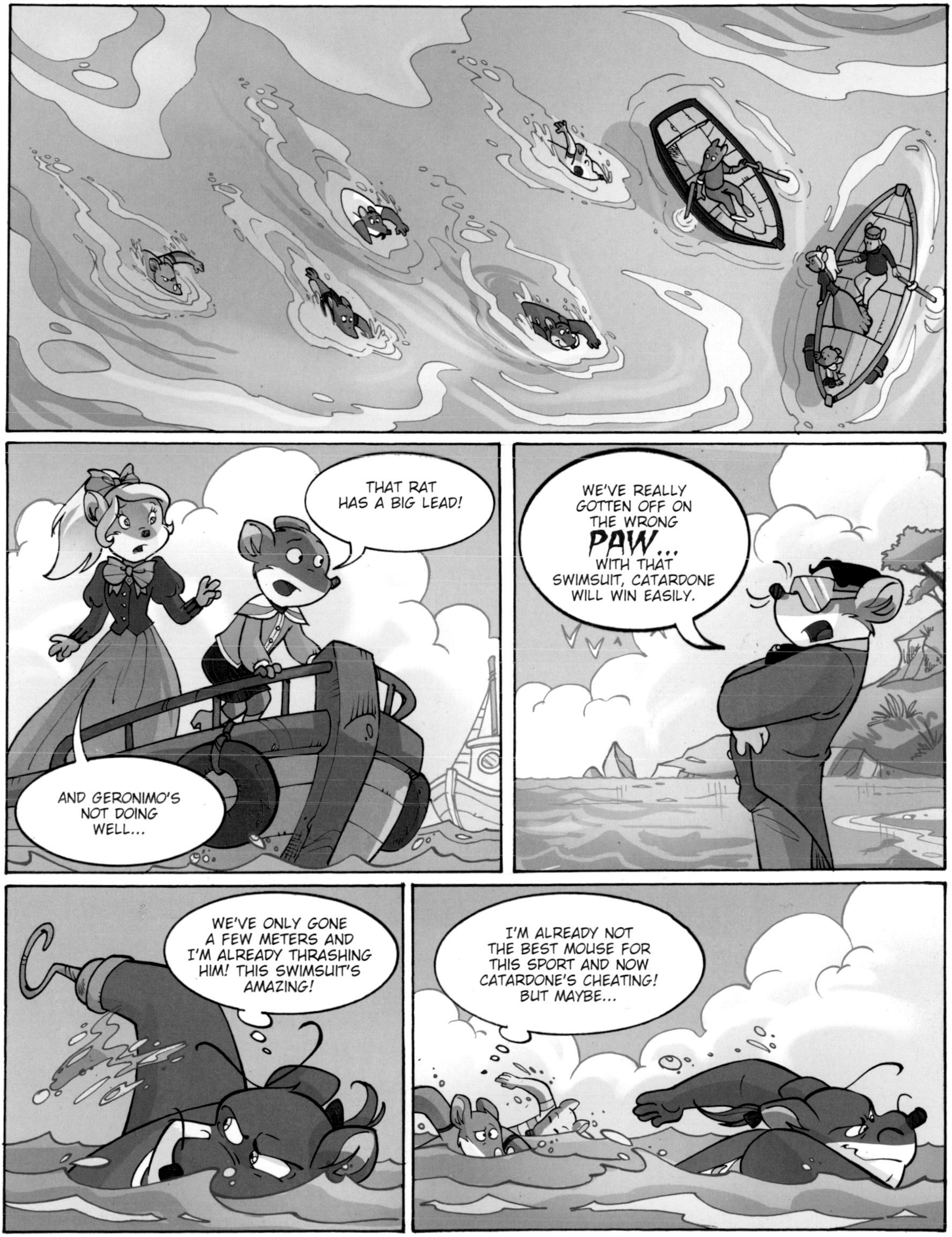
THAT RAT HAS A BIG LEAD!
AND GERONIMO'S NOT DOING WELL...
WE'VE REALLY GOTTEN OFF ON THE WRONG PAW... WITH THAT SWIMSUIT, CATARDONE WILL WIN EASILY.
WE'VE ONLY GONE A FEW METERS AND I'M ALREADY THRASHING HIM! THIS SWIMSUIT'S AMAZING!
I'M ALREADY NOT THE BEST MOUSE FOR THIS SPORT AND NOW CATARDONE'S CHEATING! BUT MAYBE...

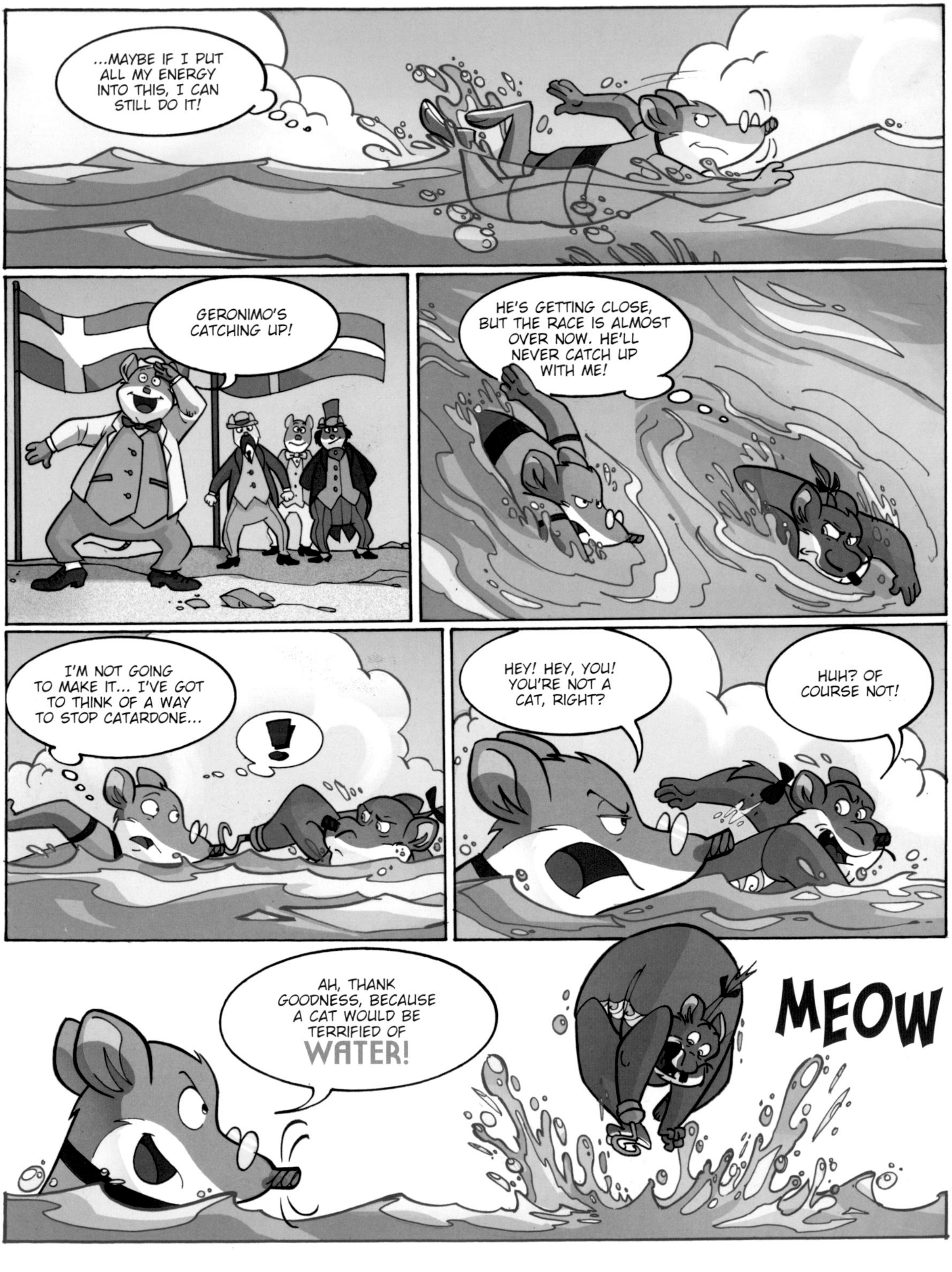
...MAYBE IF I PUT ALL MY ENERGY INTO THIS, I CAN STILL DO IT!
GERONIMO'S CATCHING UP!
HE'S GETTING CLOSE, BUT THE RACE IS ALMOST OVER NOW. HE'LL NEVER CATCH UP WITH ME!
I'M NOT GOING TO MAKE IT... I'VE GOT TO THINK OF A WAY TO STOP CATARDONE...
!
HEY! HEY, YOU! YOU'RE NOT A CAT, RIGHT?
HUH? OF COURSE NOT!
AH, THANK GOODNESS, BECAUSE A CAT WOULD BE TERRIFIED OF WATER!
MEOW

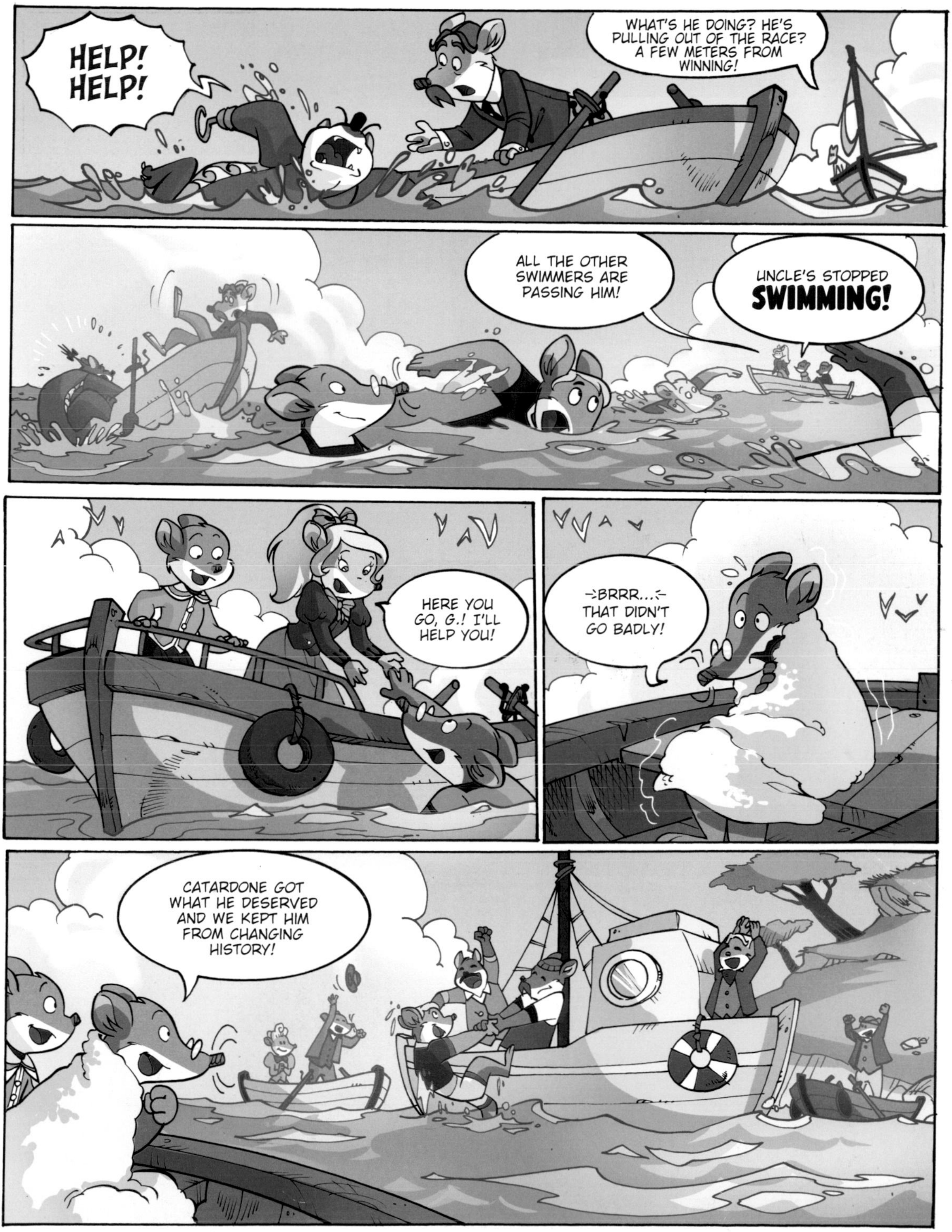
HELP! HELP!
WHAT'S HE DOING? HE'S PULLING OUT OF THE RACE? A FEW METERS FROM WINNING!
ALL THE OTHER SWIMMERS ARE PASSING HIM!
UNCLE'S STOPPED SWIMMING!
HERE YOU GO, G.! I'LL HELP YOU!
BRRR... THAT DIDN'T GO BADLY!
CATARDONE GOT WHAT HE DESERVED AND WE KEPT HIM FROM CHANGING HISTORY!

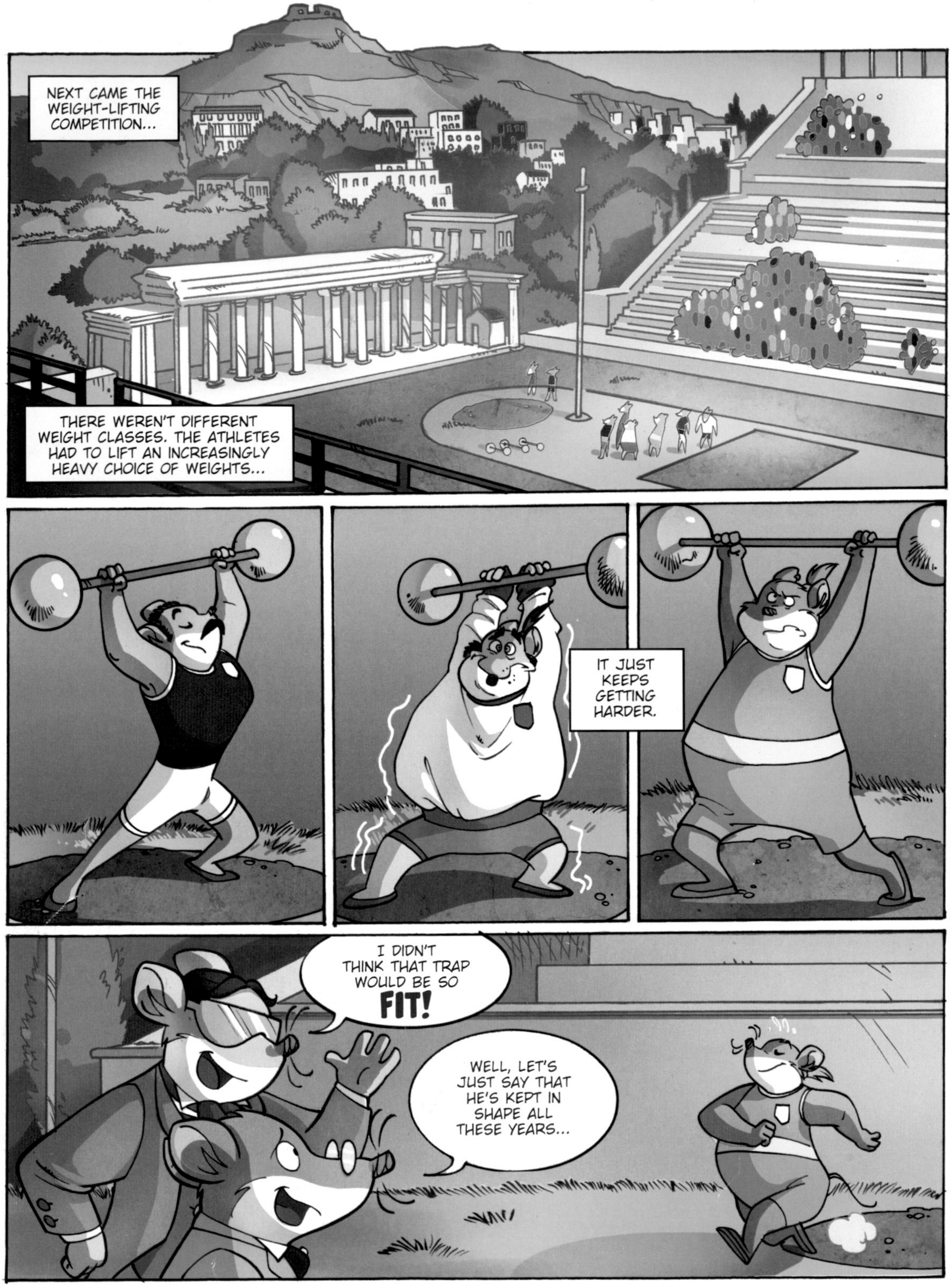
NEXT CAME THE WEIGHT-LIFTING COMPETITION...
THERE WEREN'T DIFFERENT WEIGHT CLASSES. THE ATHLETES HAD TO LIFT AN INCREASINGLY HEAVY CHOICE OF WEIGHTS...
IT JUST KEEPS GETTING HARDER.
I DIDN'T THINK THAT TRAP WOULD BE SO FIT!
WELL, LET'S JUST SAY THAT HE'S KEPT IN SHAPE ALL THESE YEARS...

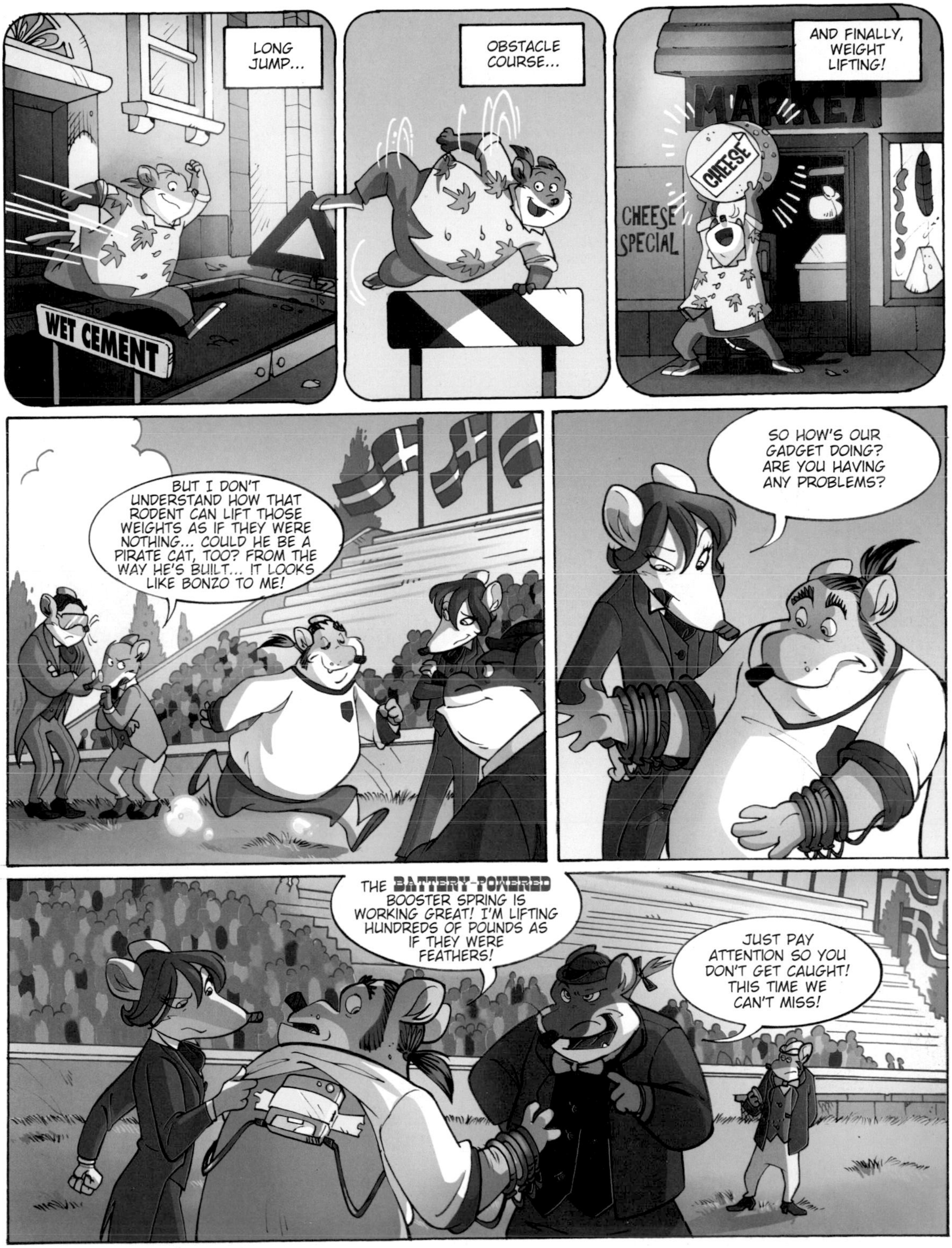
LONG JUMP...
WET CEMENT
OBSTACLE COURSE...
AND FINALLY, WEIGHT LIFTING!
MARKET
CHEESE
CHEESE SPECIAL
BUT I DON'T UNDERSTAND HOW THAT RODENT CAN LIFT THOSE WEIGHTS AS IF THEY WERE NOTHING... COULD HE BE A PIRATE CAT, TOO? FROM THE WAY HE'S BUILT... IT LOOKS LIKE BONZO TO ME!
SO HOW'S OUR GADGET DOING? ARE YOU HAVING ANY PROBLEMS?
THE BATTERY-POWERED BOOSTER SPRING IS WORKING GREAT! I'M LIFTING HUNDREDS OF POUNDS AS IF THEY WERE FEATHERS!
JUST PAY ATTENTION SO YOU DON'T GET CAUGHT! THIS TIME WE CAN'T MISS!

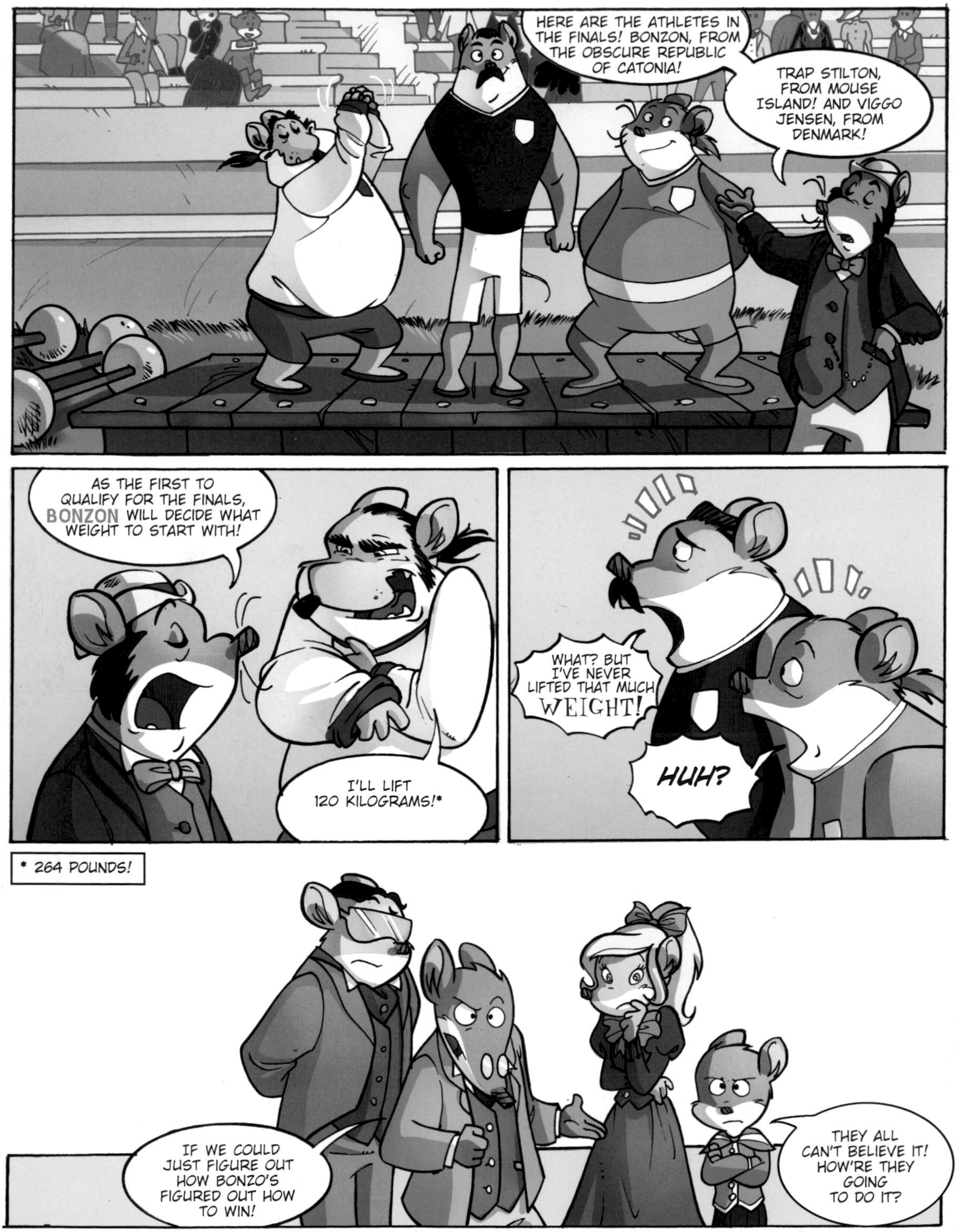
HERE ARE THE ATHLETES IN THE FINALS! BONZON, FROM THE OBSCURE REPUBLIC OF CATONIA!
TRAP STILTON, FROM MOUSE ISLAND! AND VIGGO JENSEN, FROM DENMARK!
AS THE FIRST TO QUALIFY FOR THE FINALS, BONZON WILL DECIDE WHAT WEIGHT TO START WITH!
I'LL LIFT 120 KILOGRAMS!*
WHAT? BUT I'VE NEVER LIFTED THAT MUCH WEIGHT!
HUH?
* 264 POUNDS!
IF WE COULD JUST FIGURE OUT HOW BONZO'S FIGURED OUT HOW TO WIN!
THEY ALL CAN'T BELIEVE IT! HOW'RE THEY GOING TO DO IT?

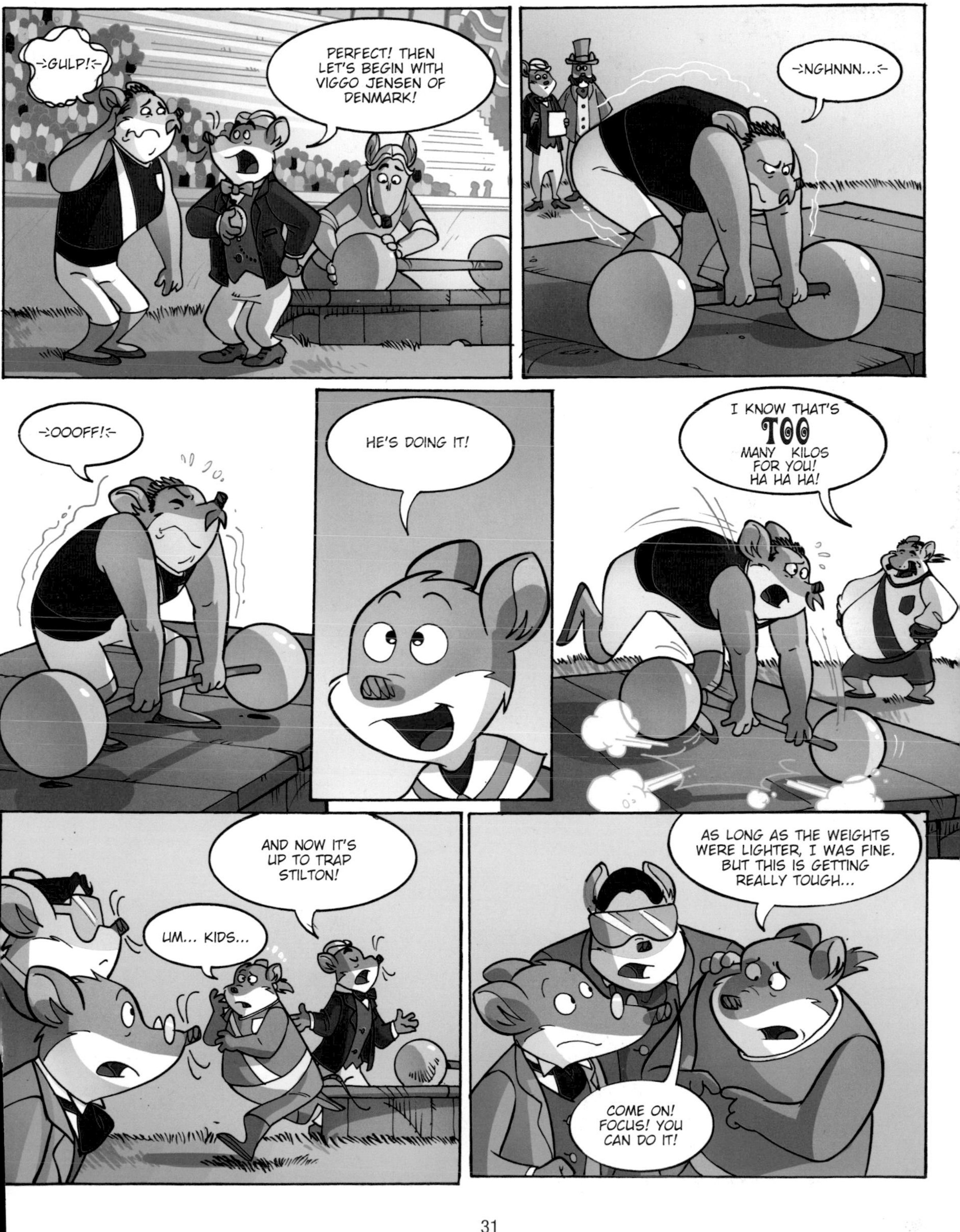

-GULP!-
PERFECT! THEN LET'S BEGIN WITH VIGGO JENSEN OF DENMARK!
-NGHNNN...-
-OOOFF!-
HE'S DOING IT!
I KNOW THAT'S TOO MANY KILOS FOR YOU! HA HA HA!
AND NOW IT'S UP TO TRAP STILTON!
UM... KIDS...
AS LONG AS THE WEIGHTS WERE LIGHTER, I WAS FINE. BUT THIS IS GETTING REALLY TOUGH...
COME ON! FOCUS! YOU CAN DO IT!

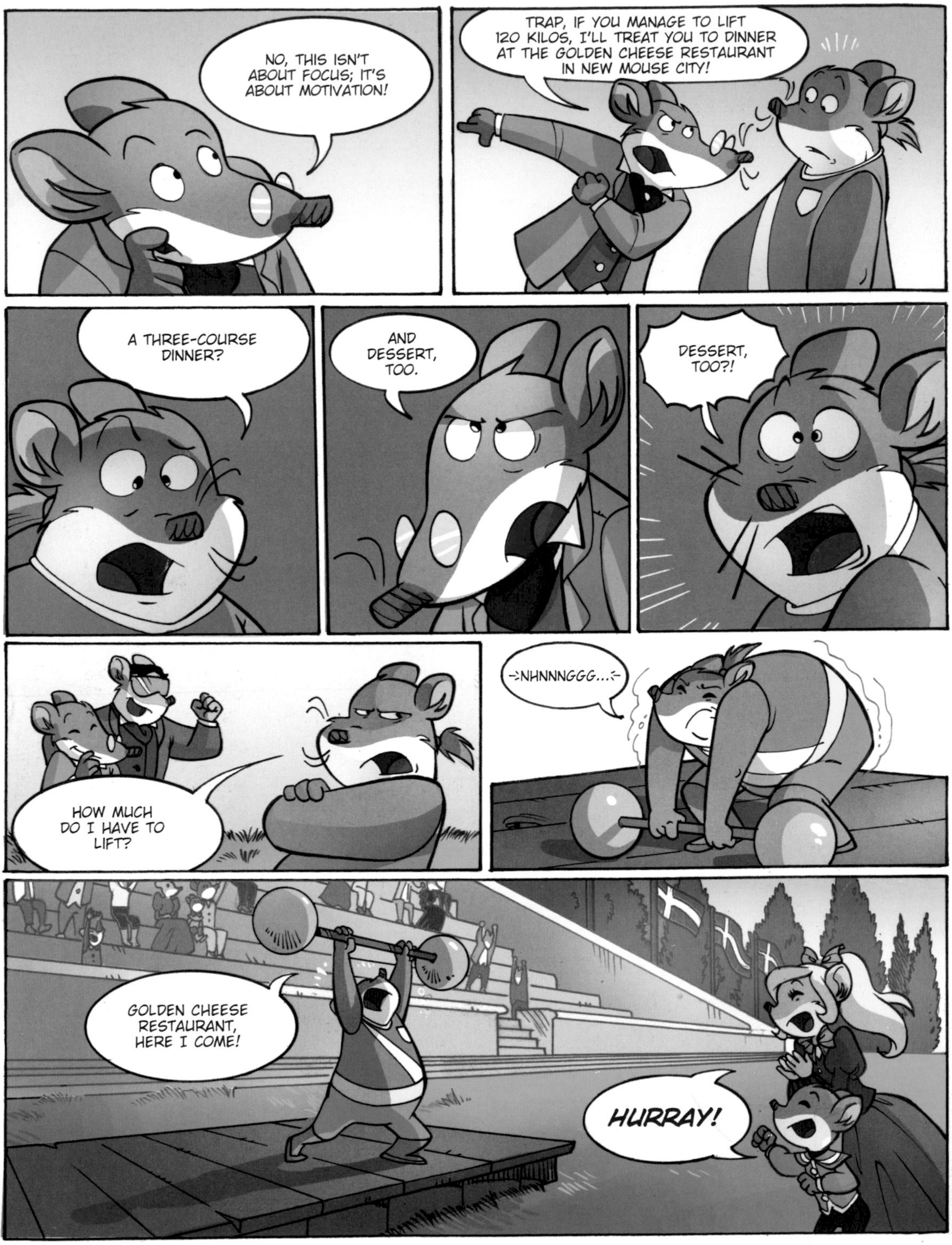
NO, THIS ISN'T ABOUT FOCUS; IT'S ABOUT MOTIVATION!
TRAP, IF YOU MANAGE TO LIFT 120 KILOS, I'LL TREAT YOU TO DINNER AT THE GOLDEN CHEESE RESTAURANT IN NEW MOUSE CITY!
A THREE-COURSE DINNER?
AND DESSERT, TOO.
DESSERT, TOO?!
HOW MUCH DO I HAVE TO LIFT?
NHNNNGGG...
GOLDEN CHEESE RESTAURANT, HERE I COME!
HURRAY!

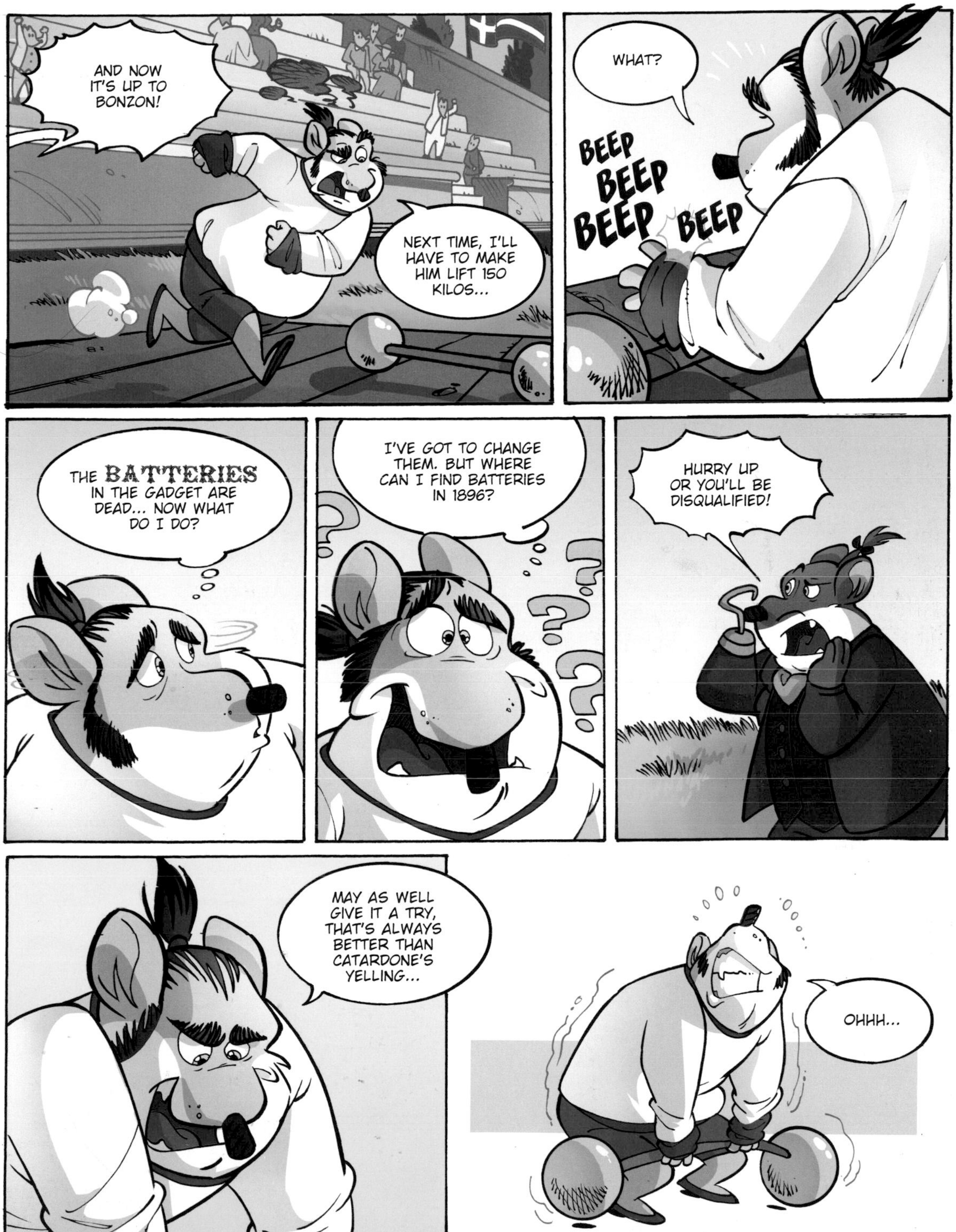
AND NOW IT'S UP TO BONZON!
NEXT TIME, I'LL HAVE TO MAKE HIM LIFT 150 KILOS...
WHAT?
BEEP BEEP BEEP BEEP
THE BATTERIES IN THE GADGET ARE DEAD... NOW WHAT DO I DO?
I'VE GOT TO CHANGE THEM. BUT WHERE CAN I FIND BATTERIES IN 1896?
HURRY UP OR YOU'LL BE DISQUALIFIED!
MAY AS WELL GIVE IT A TRY, THAT'S ALWAYS BETTER THAN CATARDONE'S YELLING...
OHHH...

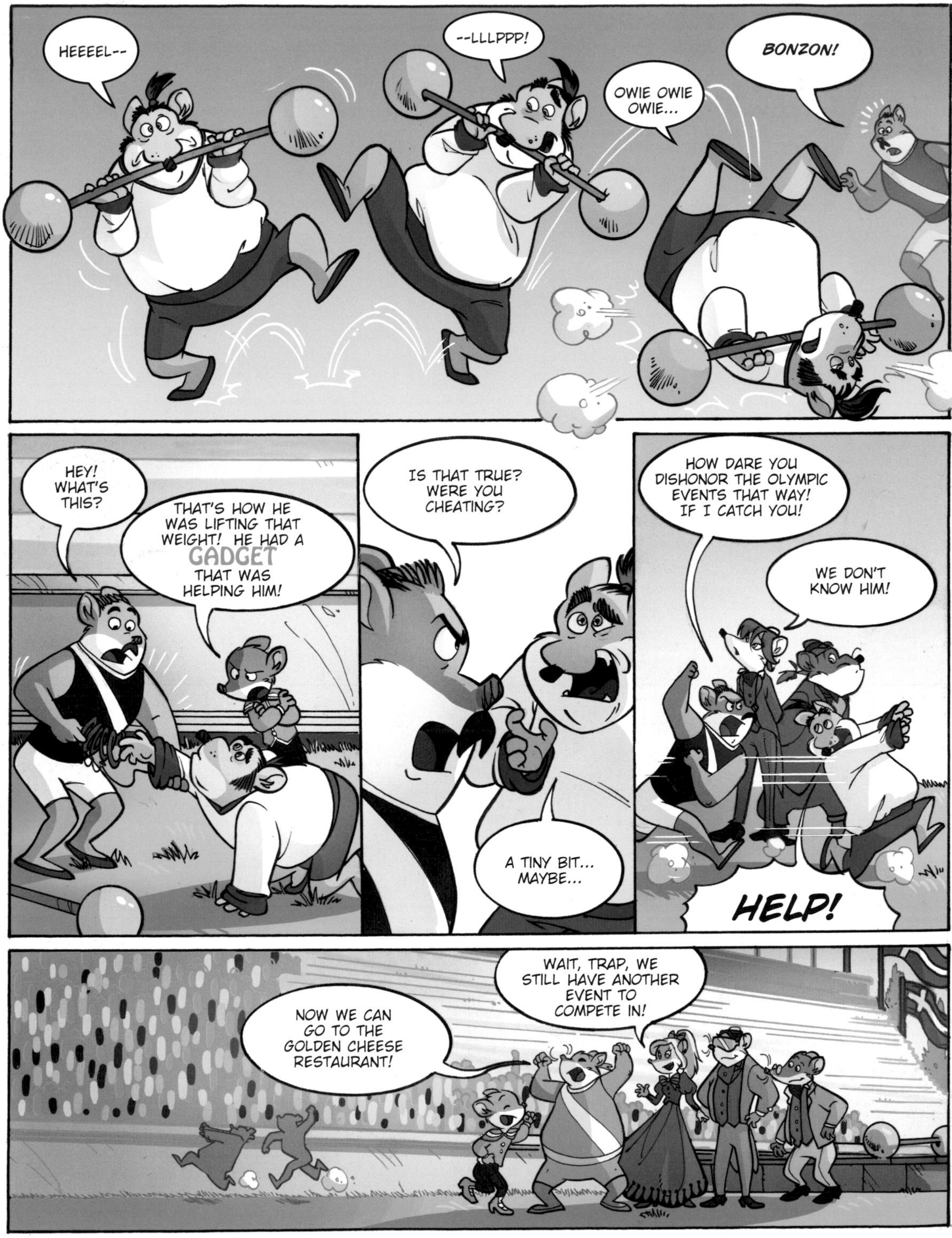
HEEEEL--
--LLLPPP!
OWIE OWIE OWIE...
BONZON!
HEY! WHAT'S THIS?
THAT'S HOW HE WAS LIFTING THAT WEIGHT! HE HAD A GADGET THAT WAS HELPING HIM!
IS THAT TRUE? WERE YOU CHEATING?
A TINY BIT... MAYBE...
HOW DARE YOU DISHONOR THE OLYMPIC EVENTS THAT WAY! IF I CATCH YOU!
WE DON'T KNOW HIM!
HELP!
NOW WE CAN GO TO THE GOLDEN CHEESE RESTAURANT!
WAIT, TRAP, WE STILL HAVE ANOTHER EVENT TO COMPETE IN!

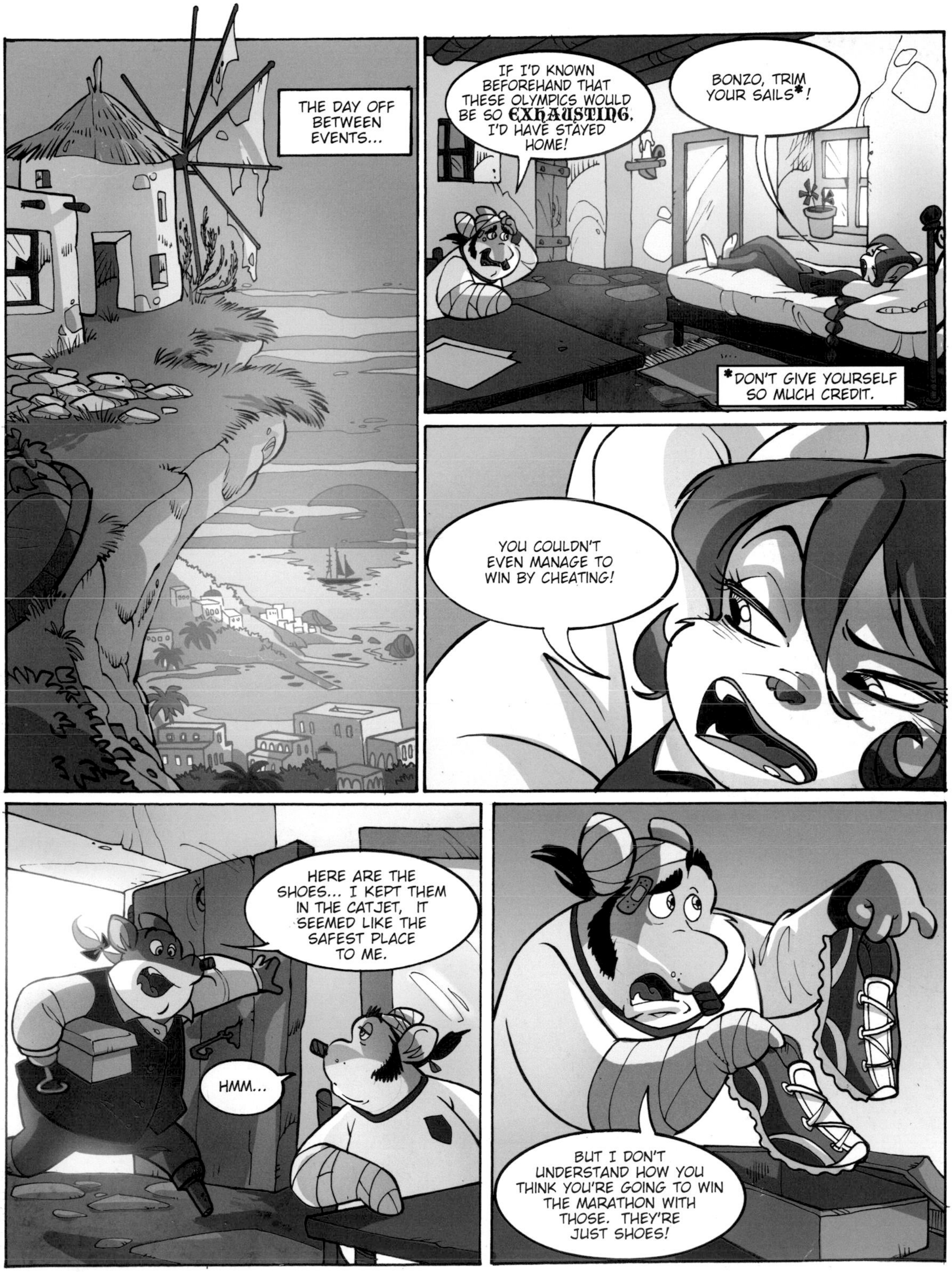
THE DAY OFF BETWEEN EVENTS...
IF I'D KNOWN BEFOREHAND THAT THESE OLYMPICS WOULD BE SO EXHAUSTING, I'D HAVE STAYED HOME!
BONZO, TRIM YOUR SAILS*!
*DON'T GIVE YOURSELF SO MUCH CREDIT.
YOU COULDN'T EVEN MANAGE TO WIN BY CHEATING!
HERE ARE THE SHOES... I KEPT THEM IN THE CATJET, IT SEEMED LIKE THE SAFEST PLACE TO ME.
HMM...
BUT I DON'T UNDERSTAND HOW YOU THINK YOU'RE GOING TO WIN THE MARATHON WITH THOSE. THEY'RE JUST SHOES!

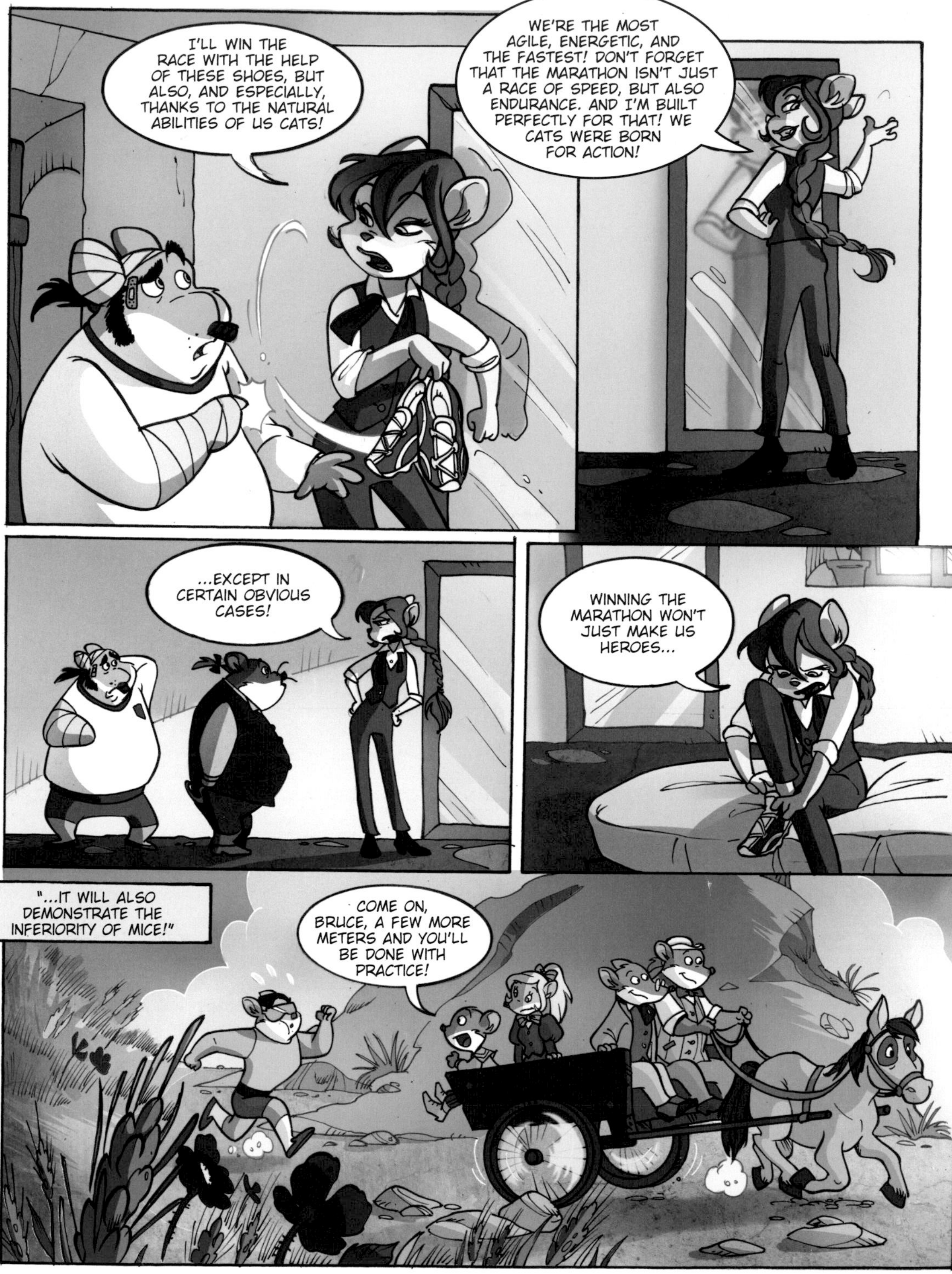
I'LL WIN THE RACE WITH THE HELP OF THESE SHOES, BUT ALSO, AND ESPECIALLY, THANKS TO THE NATURAL ABILITIES OF US CATS!
WE'RE THE MOST AGILE, ENERGETIC, AND THE FASTEST! DON'T FORGET THAT THE MARATHON ISN'T JUST A RACE OF SPEED, BUT ALSO ENDURANCE. AND I'M BUILT PERFECTLY FOR THAT! WE CATS WERE BORN FOR ACTION!
...EXCEPT IN CERTAIN OBVIOUS CASES!
WINNING THE MARATHON WON'T JUST MAKE US HEROES...
"...IT WILL ALSO DEMONSTRATE THE INFERIORITY OF MICE!"
COME ON, BRUCE, A FEW MORE METERS AND YOU'LL BE DONE WITH PRACTICE!

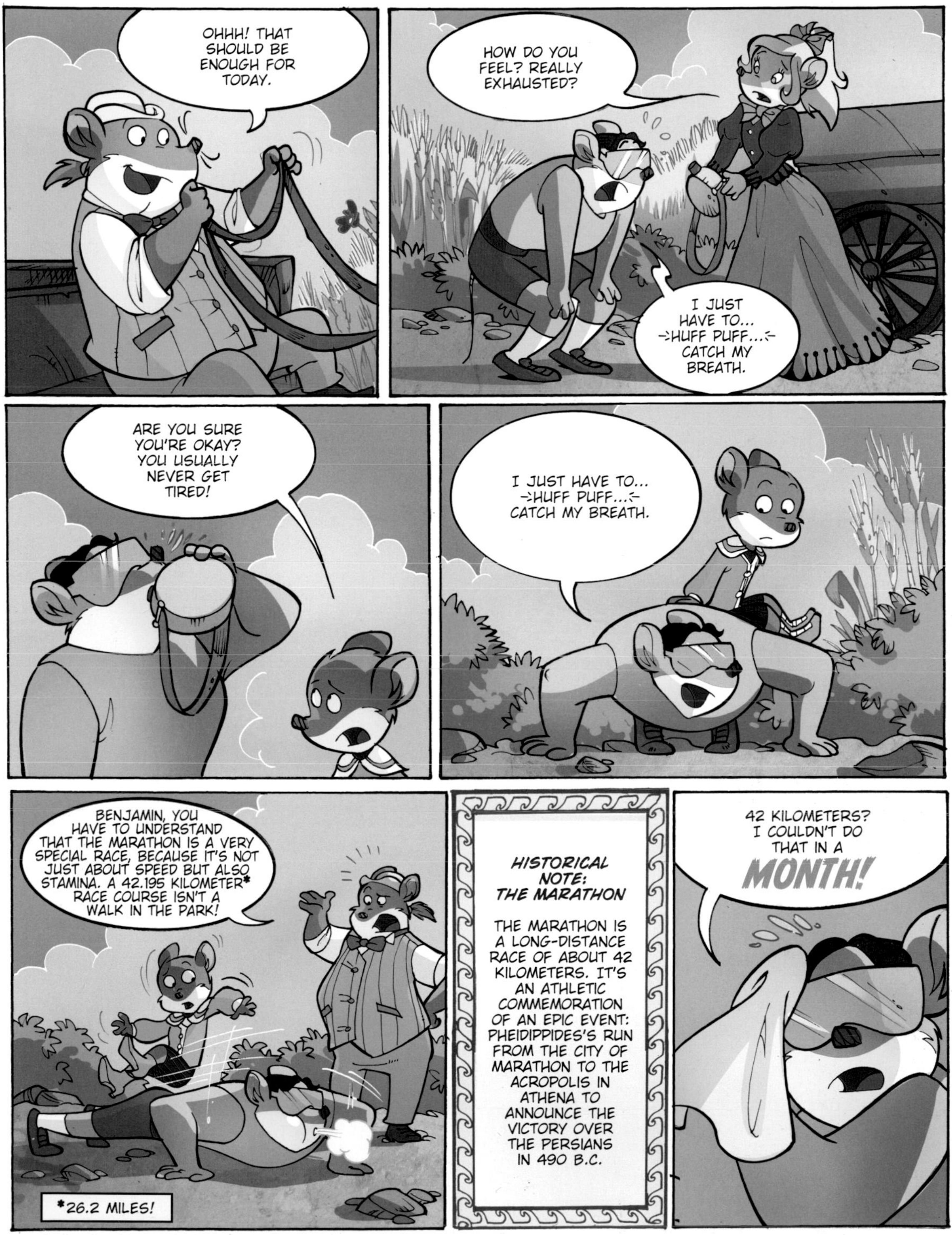
OHHH! THAT SHOULD BE ENOUGH FOR TODAY.
HOW DO YOU FEEL? REALLY EXHAUSTED?
I JUST HAVE TO... -HUFF PUFF...- CATCH MY BREATH.
ARE YOU SURE YOU'RE OKAY? YOU USUALLY NEVER GET TIRED!
I JUST HAVE TO... -HUFF PUFF...- CATCH MY BREATH.
BENJAMIN, YOU HAVE TO UNDERSTAND THAT THE MARATHON IS A VERY SPECIAL RACE, BECAUSE IT'S NOT JUST ABOUT SPEED BUT ALSO STAMINA. A 42.195 KILOMETER* RACE COURSE ISN'T A WALK IN THE PARK!
*26.2 MILES!
HISTORICAL NOTE: THE MARATHON
THE MARATHON IS A LONG-DISTANCE RACE OF ABOUT 42 KILOMETERS. IT'S AN ATHLETIC COMMEMORATION OF AN EPIC EVENT: PHEIDIPPIDES'S RUN FROM THE CITY OF MARATHON TO THE ACROPOLIS IN ATHENA TO ANNOUNCE THE VICTORY OVER THE PERSIANS IN 490 B.C.
42 KILOMETERS? I COULDN'T DO THAT IN A MONTH!

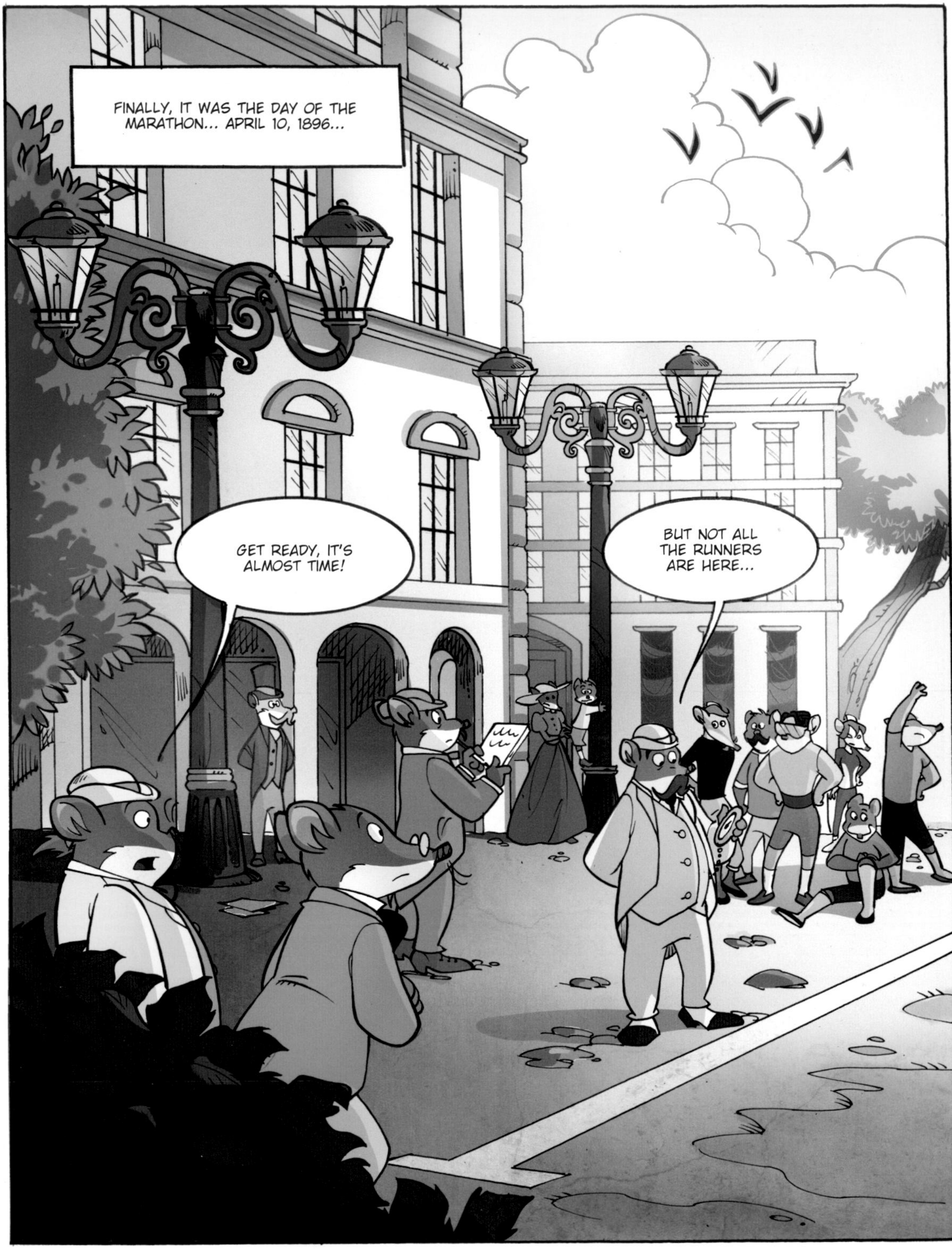
FINALLY, IT WAS THE DAY OF THE MARATHON... APRIL 10, 1896...
GET READY, IT'S ALMOST TIME!
BUT NOT ALL THE RUNNERS ARE HERE...

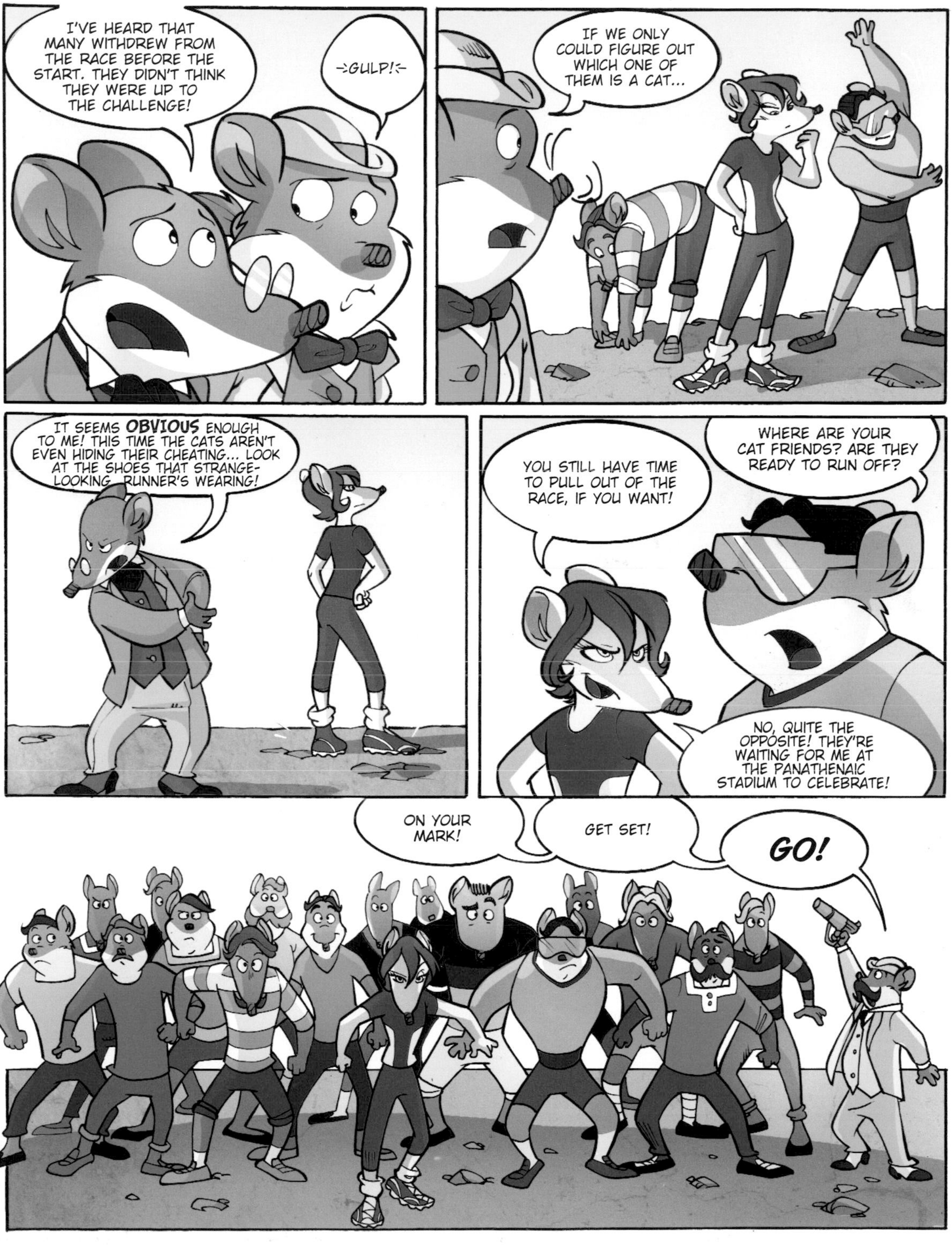

I'VE HEARD THAT MANY WITHDREW FROM THE RACE BEFORE THE START. THEY DIDN'T THINK THEY WERE UP TO THE CHALLENGE!
GULP!
IF WE ONLY COULD FIGURE OUT WHICH ONE OF THEM IS A CAT...
IT SEEMS OBVIOUS ENOUGH TO ME! THIS TIME THE CATS AREN'T EVEN HIDING THEIR CHEATING... LOOK AT THE SHOES THAT STRANGE-LOOKING RUNNER'S WEARING!
WHERE ARE YOUR CAT FRIENDS? ARE THEY READY TO RUN OFF?
YOU STILL HAVE TIME TO PULL OUT OF THE RACE, IF YOU WANT!
NO, QUITE THE OPPOSITE! THEY'RE WAITING FOR ME AT THE PANATHENAIC STADIUM TO CELEBRATE!
ON YOUR MARK!
GET SET!
GO!

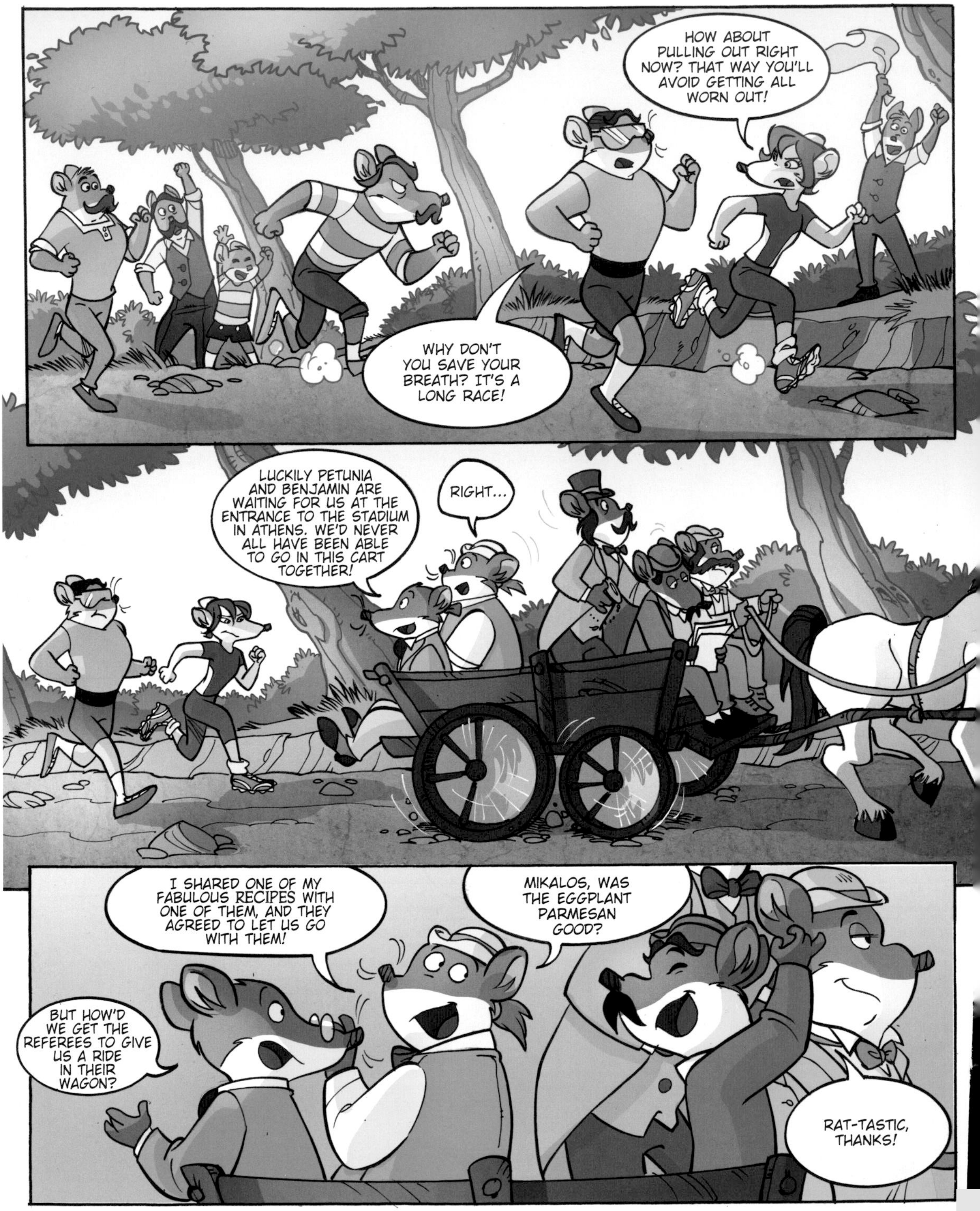
HOW ABOUT PULLING OUT RIGHT NOW? THAT WAY YOU'LL AVOID GETTING ALL WORN OUT!
WHY DON'T YOU SAVE YOUR BREATH? IT'S A LONG RACE!
LUCKILY PETUNIA AND BENJAMIN ARE WAITING FOR US AT THE ENTRANCE TO THE STADIUM IN ATHENS. WE'D NEVER ALL HAVE BEEN ABLE TO GO IN THIS CART TOGETHER!
RIGHT...
BUT HOW'D WE GET THE REFEREES TO GIVE US A RIDE IN THEIR WAGON?
I SHARED ONE OF MY FABULOUS RECIPES WITH ONE OF THEM, AND THEY AGREED TO LET US GO WITH THEM!
MIKALOS, WAS THE EGGPLANT PARMESAN GOOD?
RAT-TASTIC, THANKS!

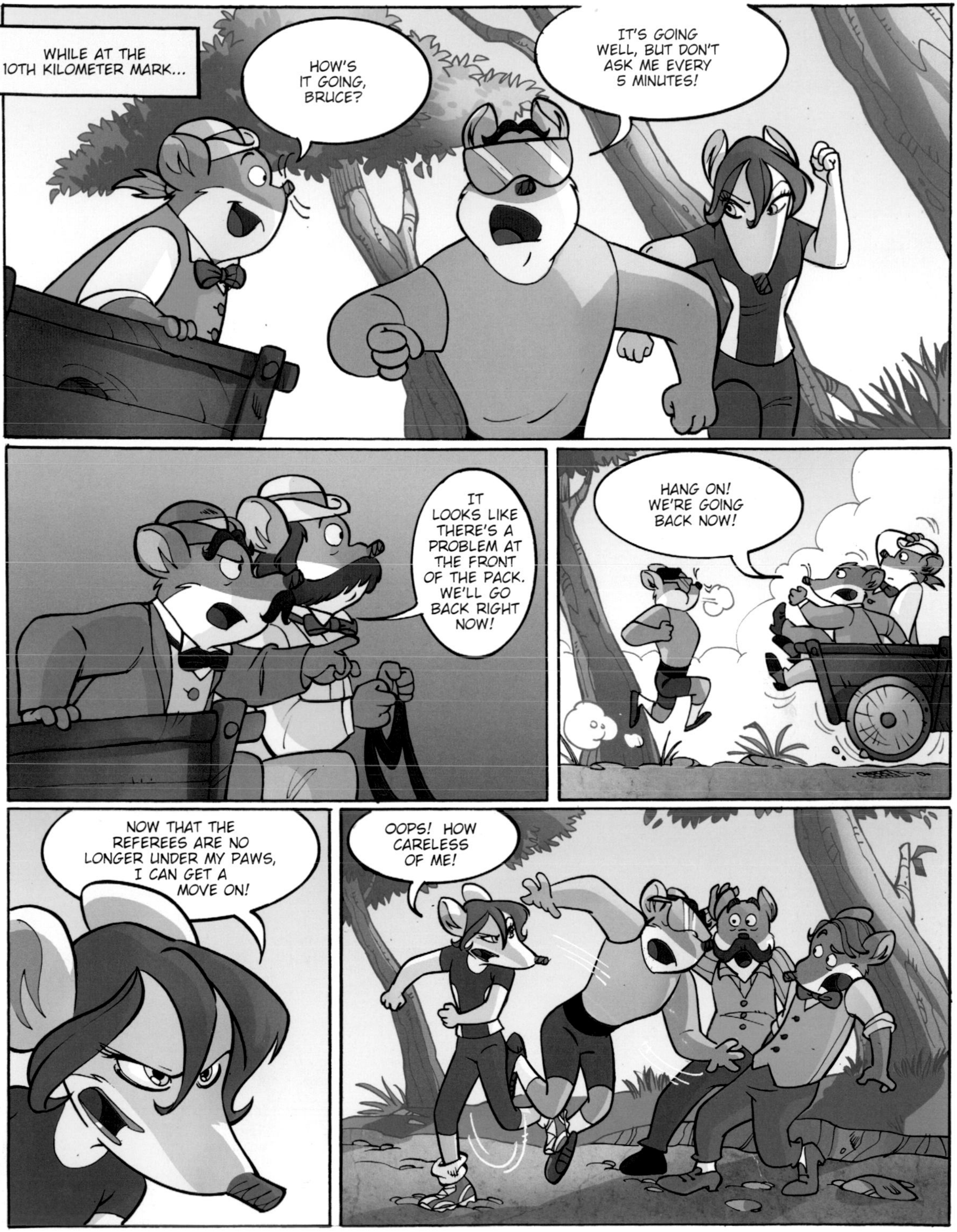
WHILE AT THE 10TH KILOMETER MARK...
HOW'S IT GOING, BRUCE?
IT'S GOING WELL, BUT DON'T ASK ME EVERY 5 MINUTES!
IT LOOKS LIKE THERE'S A PROBLEM AT THE FRONT OF THE PACK. WE'LL GO BACK RIGHT NOW!
HANG ON! WE'RE GOING BACK NOW!
NOW THAT THE REFEREES ARE NO LONGER UNDER MY PAWS, I CAN GET A MOVE ON!
OOPS! HOW CARELESS OF ME!

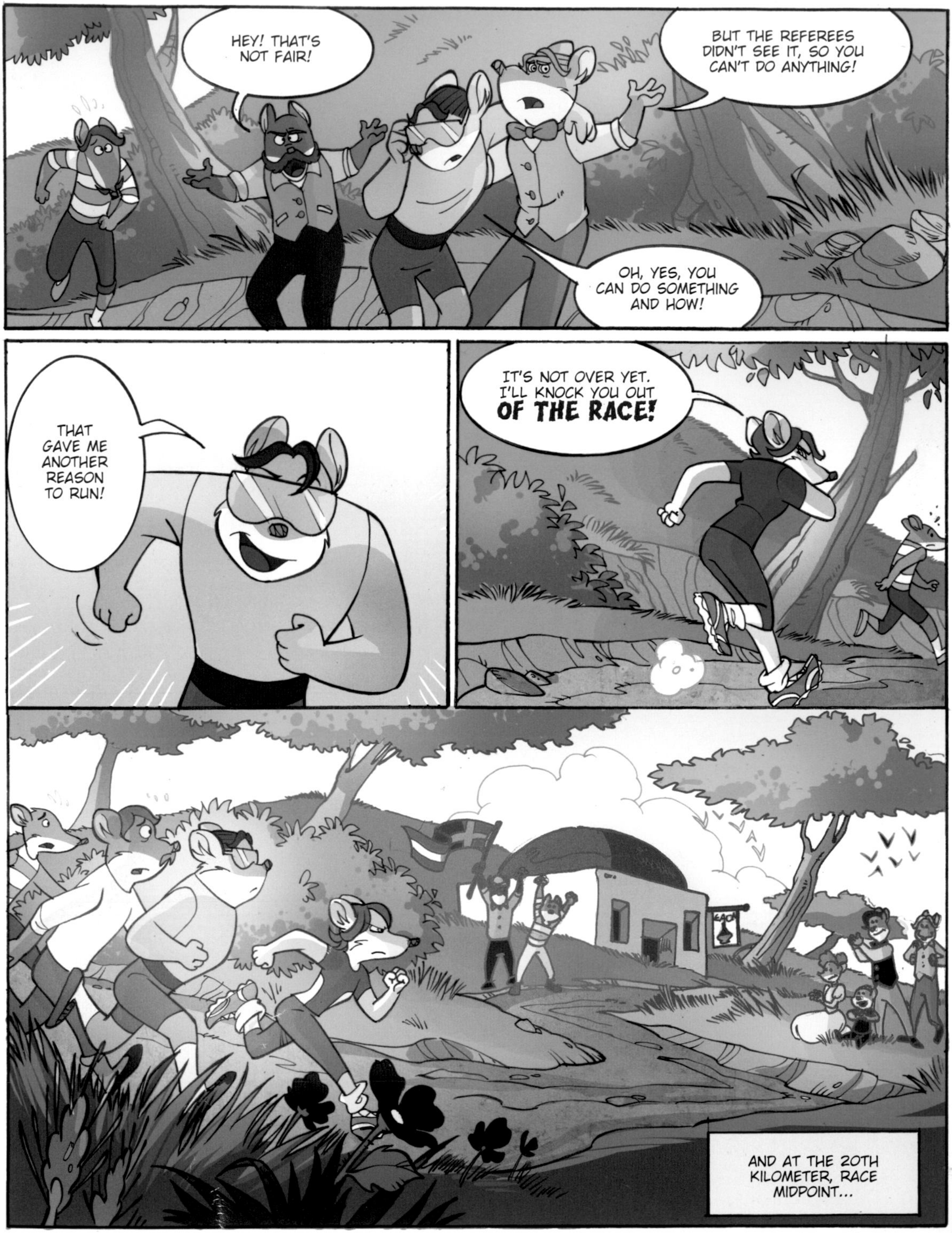

HEY! THAT'S NOT FAIR!
BUT THE REFEREES DIDN'T SEE IT, SO YOU CAN'T DO ANYTHING!
OH, YES, YOU CAN DO SOMETHING AND HOW!
THAT GAVE ME ANOTHER REASON TO RUN!
IT'S NOT OVER YET. I'LL KNOCK YOU OUT OF THE RACE!
AND AT THE 20TH KILOMETER, RACE MIDPOINT...

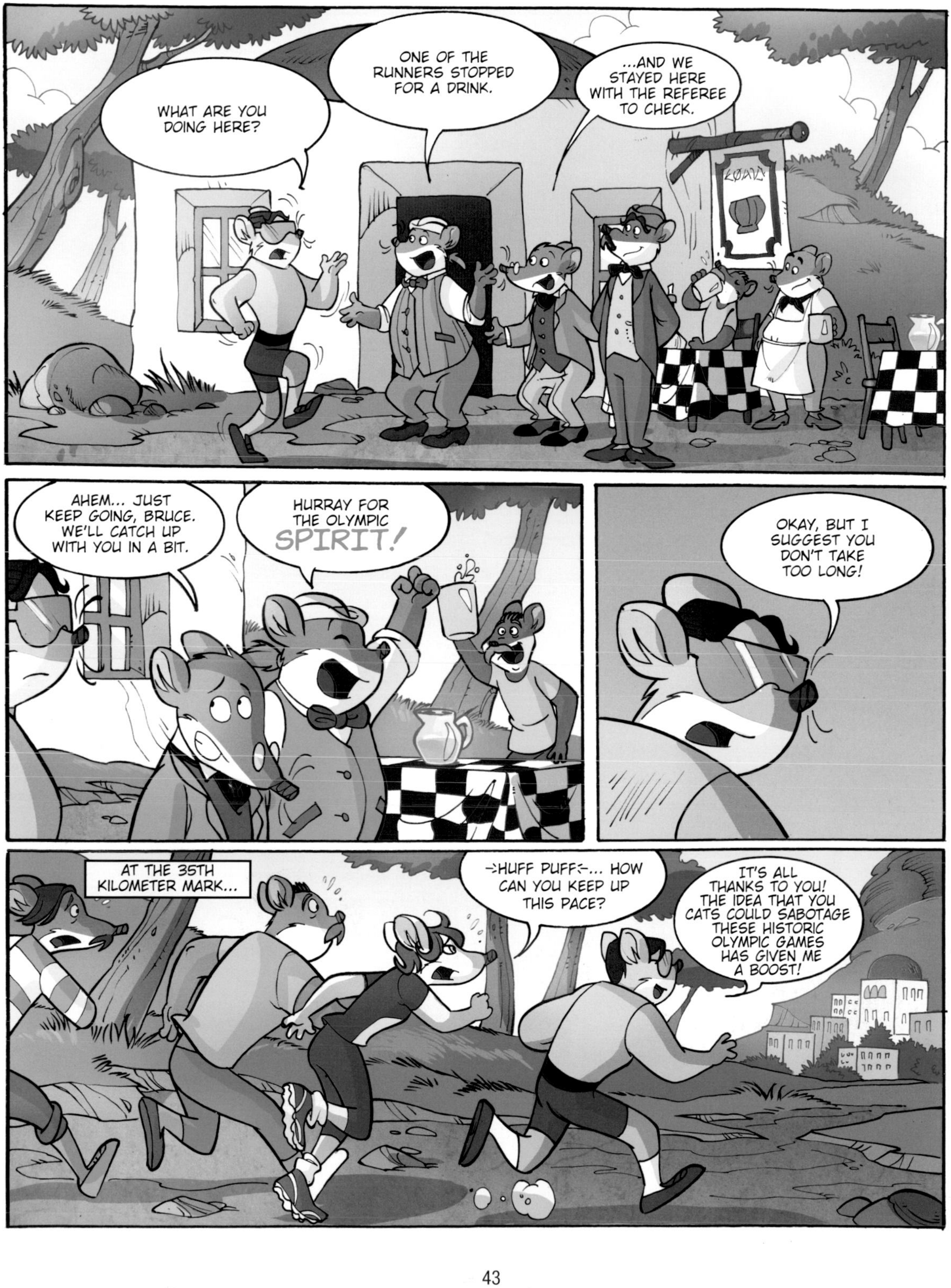
WHAT ARE YOU DOING HERE?
ONE OF THE RUNNERS STOPPED FOR A DRINK.
...AND WE STAYED HERE WITH THE REFEREE TO CHECK.
AHEM... JUST KEEP GOING, BRUCE. WE'LL CATCH UP WITH YOU IN A BIT.
HURRAY FOR THE OLYMPIC SPIRIT!
OKAY, BUT I SUGGEST YOU DON'T TAKE TOO LONG!
AT THE 35TH KILOMETER MARK...
→HUFF PUFF←... HOW CAN YOU KEEP UP THIS PACE?
IT'S ALL THANKS TO YOU! THE IDEA THAT YOU CATS COULD SABOTAGE THESE HISTORIC OLYMPIC GAMES HAS GIVEN ME A BOOST!

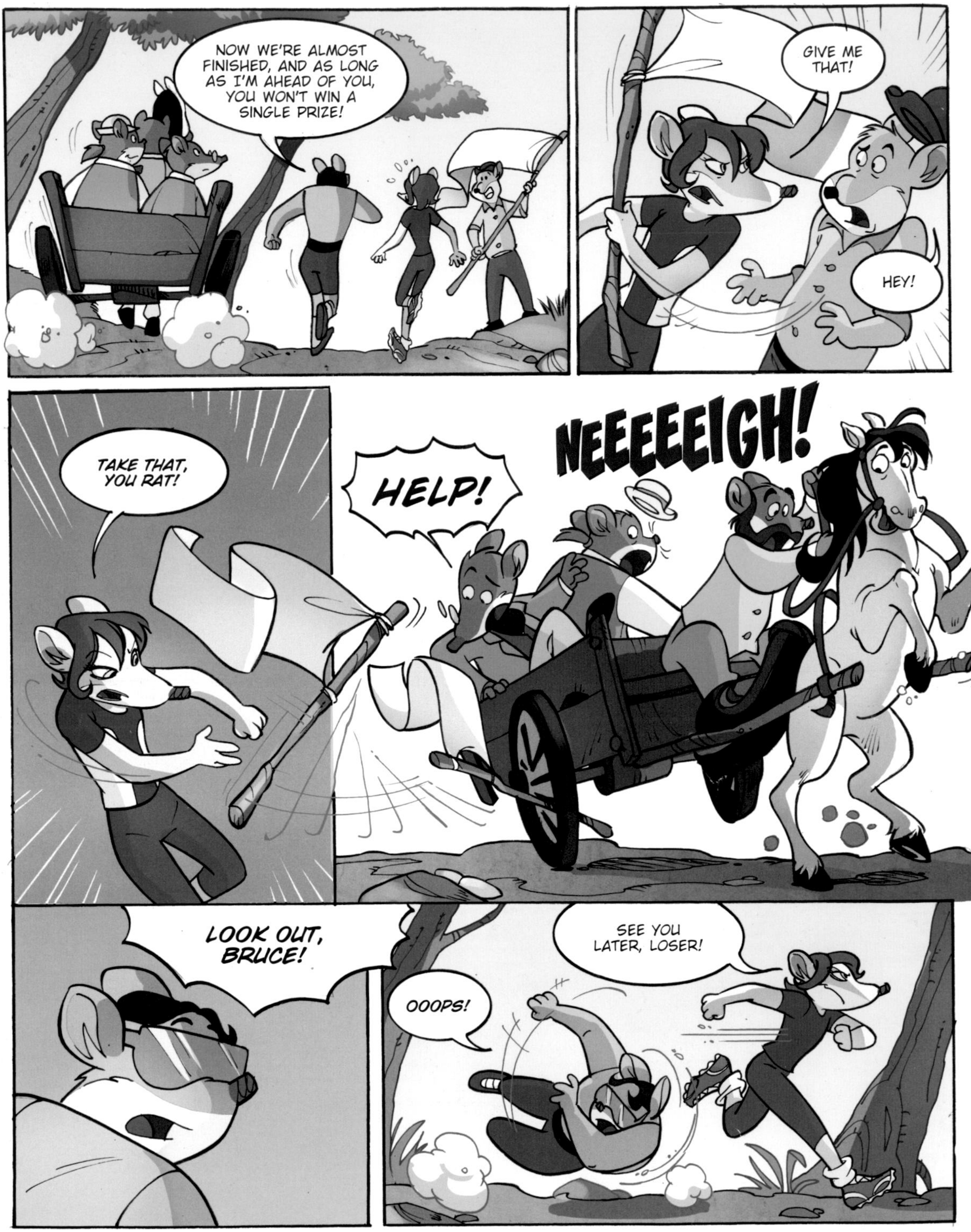
NOW WE'RE ALMOST FINISHED, AND AS LONG AS I'M AHEAD OF YOU, YOU WON'T WIN A SINGLE PRIZE!
GIVE ME THAT!
HEY!
TAKE THAT, YOU RAT!
HELP!
NEEEEEIGH!
LOOK OUT, BRUCE!
SEE YOU LATER, LOSER!
OOOPS!

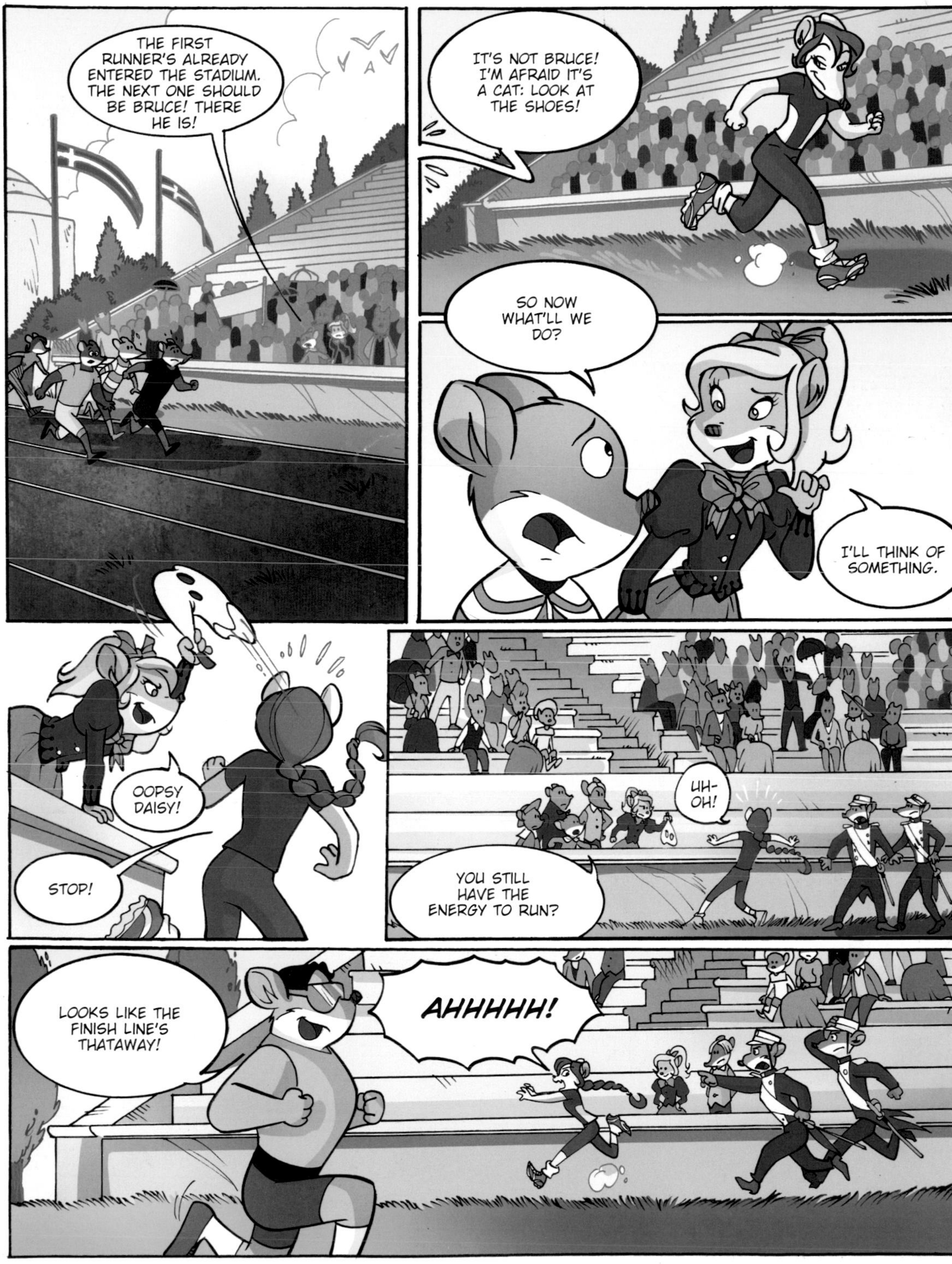
THE FIRST RUNNER'S ALREADY ENTERED THE STADIUM. THE NEXT ONE SHOULD BE BRUCE! THERE HE IS!
IT'S NOT BRUCE! I'M AFRAID IT'S A CAT: LOOK AT THE SHOES!
SO NOW WHAT'LL WE DO?
I'LL THINK OF SOMETHING.
OOPSY DAISY!
STOP!
UH-OH!
YOU STILL HAVE THE ENERGY TO RUN?
LOOKS LIKE THE FINISH LINE'S THATAWAY!
AHHHHH!

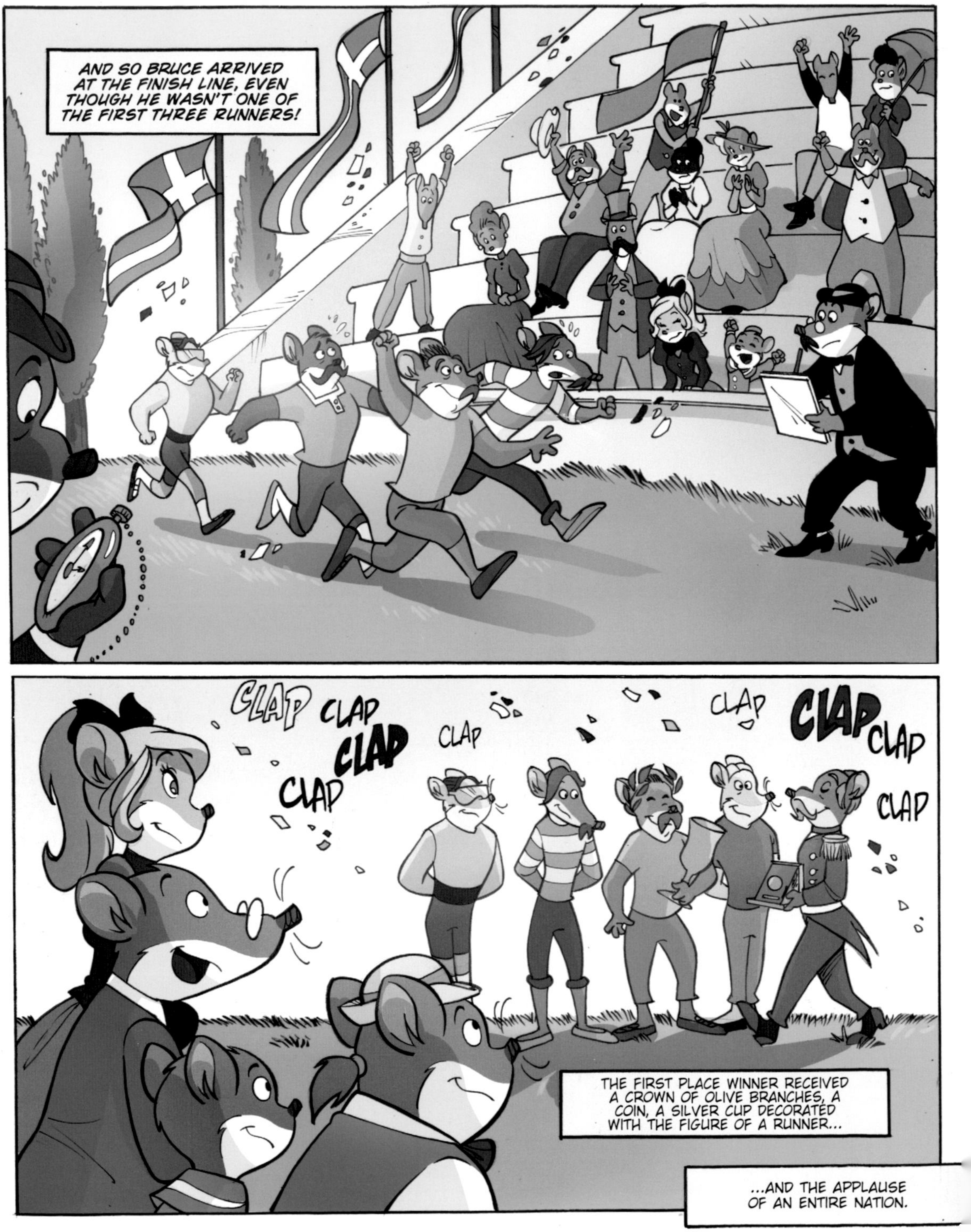
AND SO BRUCE ARRIVED AT THE FINISH LINE, EVEN THOUGH HE WASN'T ONE OF THE FIRST THREE RUNNERS!
CLAP CLAP CLAP CLAP CLAP CLAP CLAP CLAP CLAP
THE FIRST PLACE WINNER RECEIVED A CROWN OF OLIVE BRANCHES, A COIN, A SILVER CUP DECORATED WITH THE FIGURE OF A RUNNER...
...AND THE APPLAUSE OF AN ENTIRE NATION.

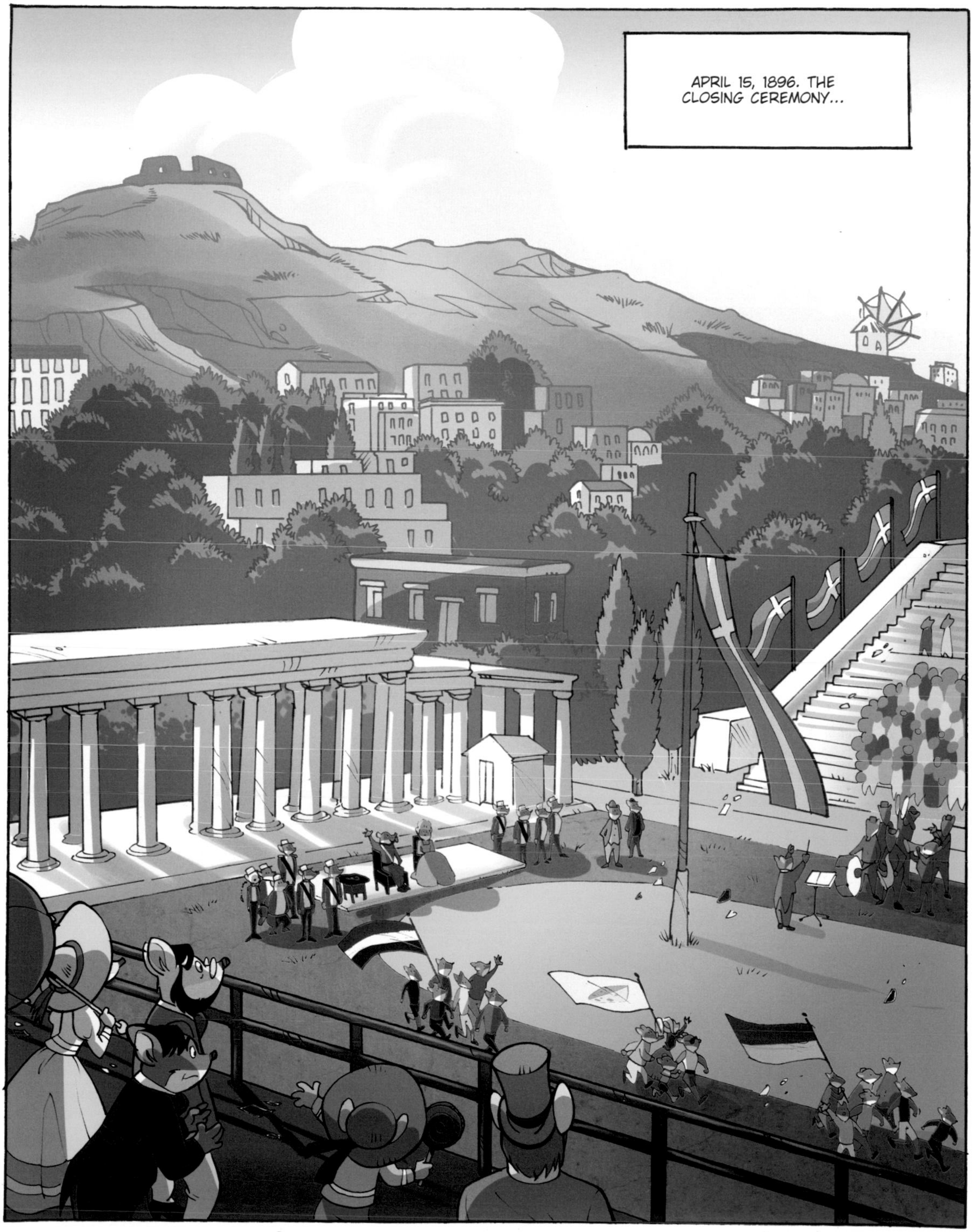
APRIL 15, 1896. THE CLOSING CEREMONY...

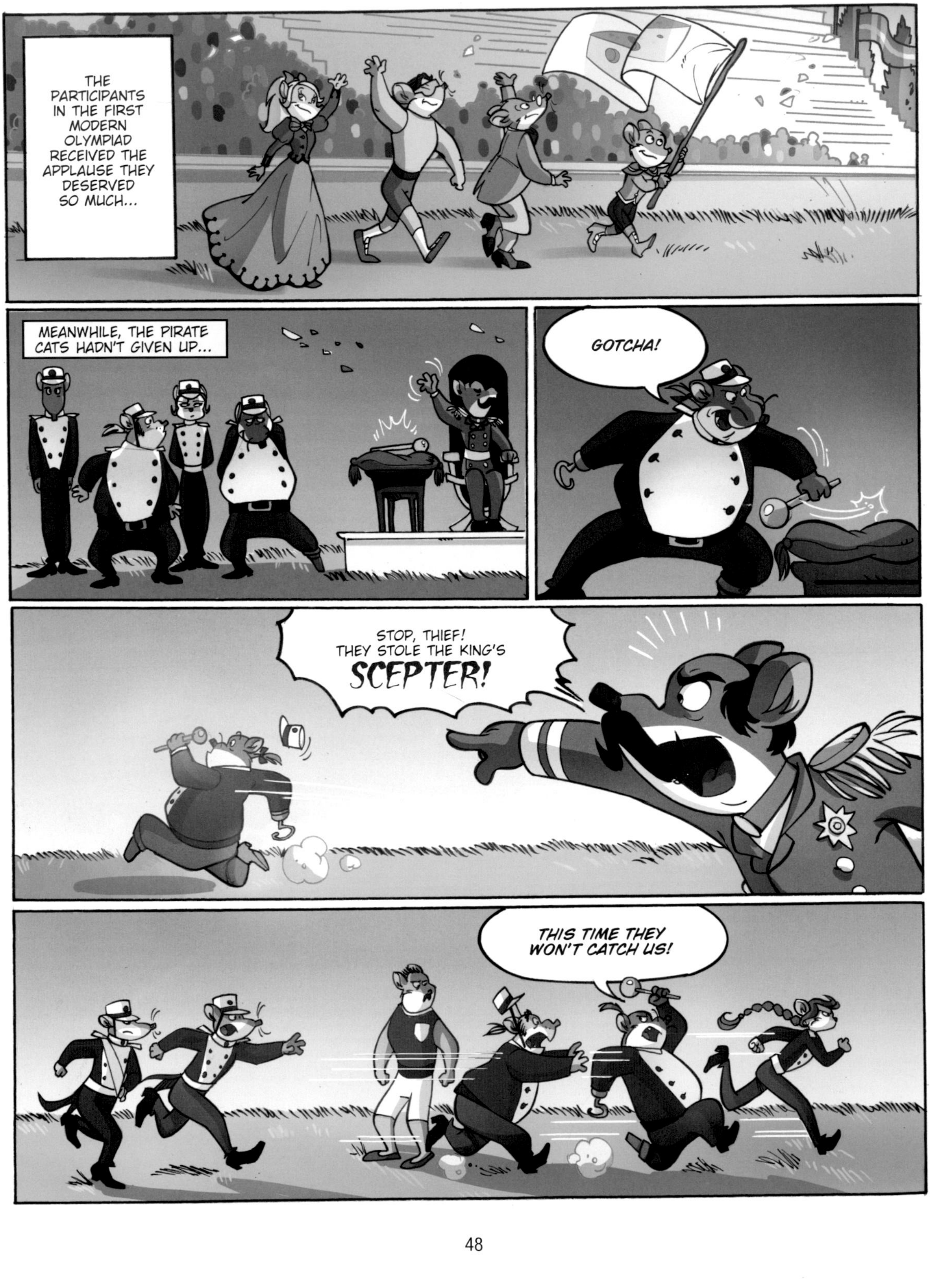

THE PARTICIPANTS IN THE FIRST MODERN OLYMPIAD RECEIVED THE APPLAUSE THEY DESERVED SO MUCH...
MEANWHILE, THE PIRATE CATS HADN'T GIVEN UP...
GOTCHA!
STOP, THIEF! THEY STOLE THE KING'S SCEPTER!
THIS TIME THEY WON'T CATCH US!

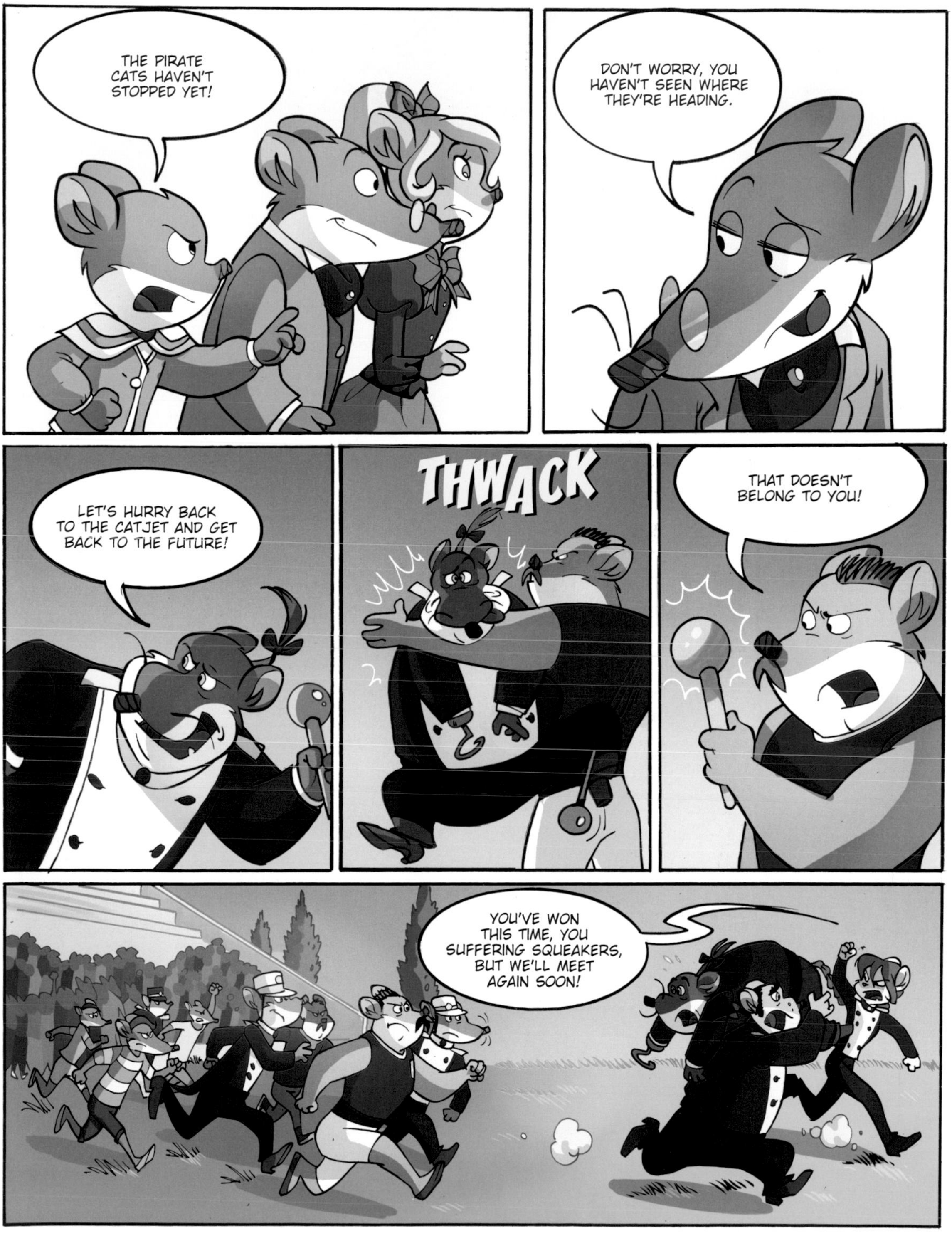
THE PIRATE CATS HAVEN'T STOPPED YET!
DON'T WORRY, YOU HAVEN'T SEEN WHERE THEY'RE HEADING.
LET'S HURRY BACK TO THE CATJET AND GET BACK TO THE FUTURE!
THWACK
THAT DOESN'T BELONG TO YOU!
YOU'VE WON THIS TIME, YOU SUFFERING SQUEAKERS, BUT WE'LL MEET AGAIN SOON!

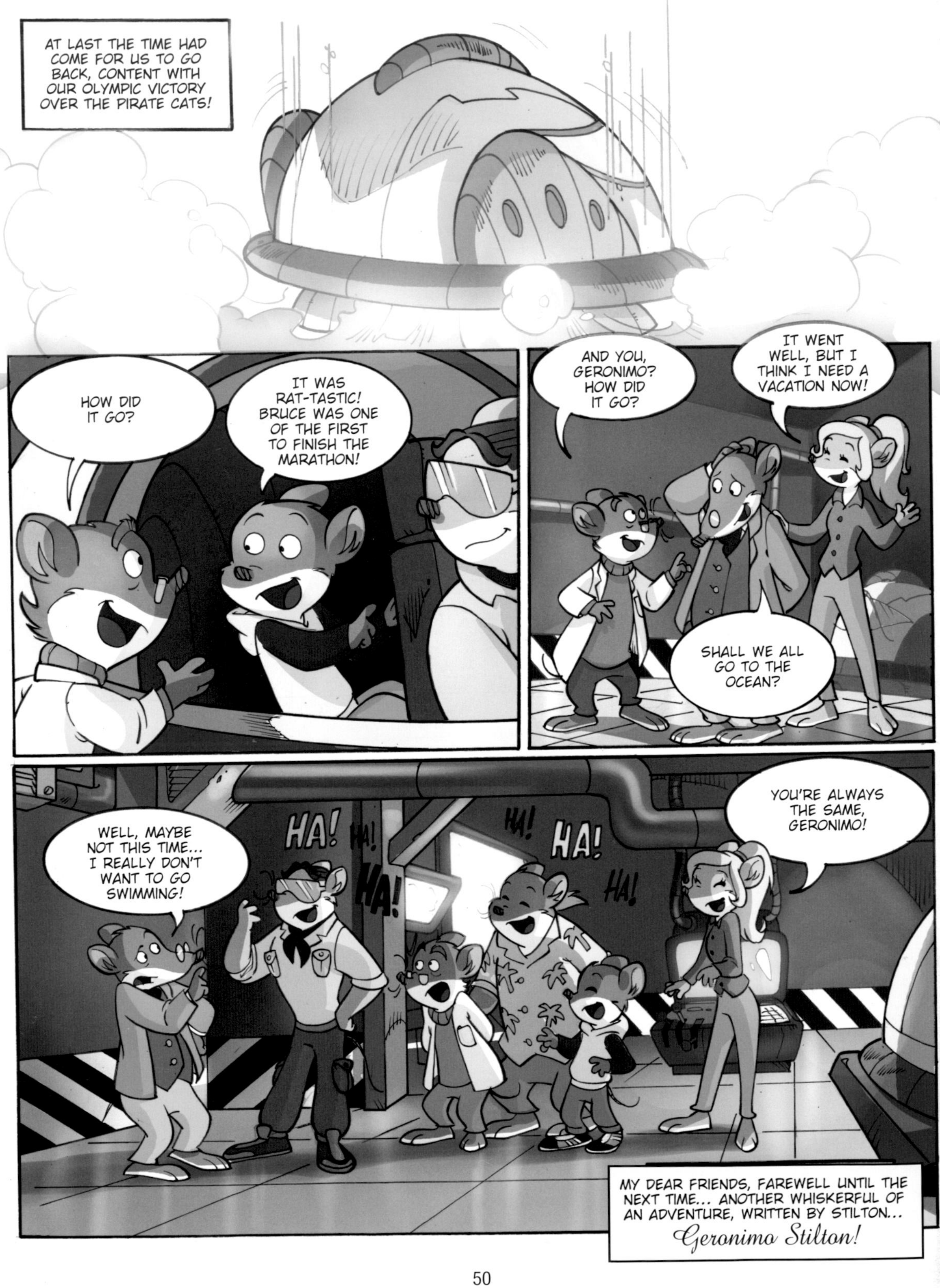

AT LAST THE TIME HAD COME FOR US TO GO BACK, CONTENT WITH OUR OLYMPIC VICTORY OVER THE PIRATE CATS!
HOW DID IT GO?
IT WAS RAT-TASTIC! BRUCE WAS ONE OF THE FIRST TO FINISH THE MARATHON!
AND YOU, GERONIMO? HOW DID IT GO?
IT WENT WELL, BUT I THINK I NEED A VACATION NOW!
SHALL WE ALL GO TO THE OCEAN?
WELL, MAYBE NOT THIS TIME... I REALLY DON'T WANT TO GO SWIMMING!
HA! HA! HA! HA! HA! HA!
YOU'RE ALWAYS THE SAME, GERONIMO!
MY DEAR FRIENDS, FAREWELL UNTIL THE NEXT TIME... ANOTHER WHISKERFUL OF AN ADVENTURE, WRITTEN BY STILTON...
Geronimo Stilton!

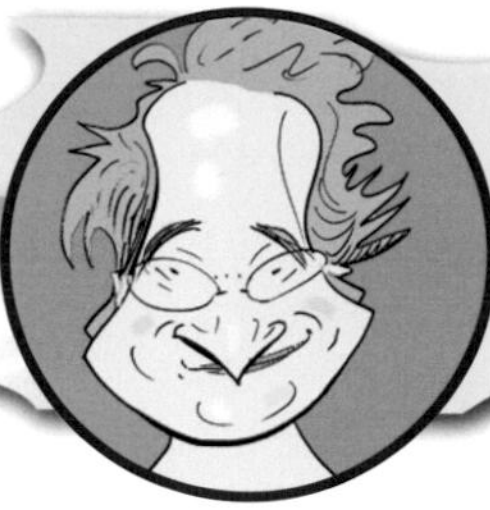

Watch Out For PAPERCUTZ

Welcome to the time-tripping tenth GERONIMO STILTON graphic novel from Papercutz—the people dedicated to publishing great graphic novels for all ages. And before I forget, allow me to introduce myself—I'm Salicrup, *Jim Salicrup* the Editor-in-Chief of Papercutz. As I was heading into our palatial offices today, I couldn't help think of how the Olympics reflect so much of life as we know it. Here are just a few of the examples…

While Papercutz is often considered the premier publisher of graphic novels for all ages, we're always in competition with every other publisher, as well as movie studio, TV network, and video game company, in vying for your attention. Like Geronimo, we're not really very big, but we are scrappy. Because we're such a tiny company compared to all those gigantic media conglomerates, we have to work extra hard just to stay in the race! What that means is, we have to make sure we're publishing characters that you love, such as GERONIMO STILTON, in the very best graphic novels we can possibly produce. In truth, we don't mind the competition, as it keeps us on our toes. And we also don't mind being the little guy— just look at how many tiny characters (THE SMURFS, DISNEY FAIRIES, ERNEST & REBECCA, GARFIELD & Co, etc.) we proudly publish at Papercutz! So, like in the Olympics, where athletes from the smallest nations compete against champions from the world's biggest countries, as long as there's a level playing field, the best will always come out on top!

Also like the Olympics, each and every GERONIMO STILTON book is the product of cooperation between different countries, although not on quite as grand a scale as the Olympics. Every GERONIMO STILTON graphic novel starts in Italy and is sent to other publishers all over the world to publish in their native languages. Papercutz publishes GERONIMO STILTON in English, thanks to the expert translating talents of Nanette McGuinness and the digital lettering skills of the mysterious Ortho. The books are then printed in China and shipped to our German-owned distributor Macmillan (and for the comicbook stores, Diamond). Eventually the GERONIMO STILTON graphic novels make their way onto the bookshelves of hundreds of bookstores (and comicbook shops), where they are finally sold to you! And you can be anyone—from anywhere! And that's what's really wonderful—that GERONIMO STILTON is such a universally appealing character, that it doesn't matter where you or your ancestors may come from, we can all equally enjoy the Editor of the Rodent's Gazette's time-travelling tales!

But just like in the real world, not everyone always gets along. So, while I hope that one day the Pirate Cats will finally see the light, and stop trying to cause trouble and just get along with Geronimo and his friends, I'm not going to hold my breath waiting! Now, I hope you don't think I'm being negative, and not being fair to the Pirate Cats, because I really do hope for peace and love everywhere! It's just that I've peeked at GERONIMO STILON #11 "We'll Always Have Paris," and I'm afraid those fiendish felines are still up to their old tricks! You can peek at GERONIMO STILTON #11 too—or at least a few preview pages, presented on the following pages. And if you like what you see, I hope you'll join us here next time, when Geronimo Stilton must save the future, by protecting the past!

Thanks, Jim

Caricature of Jim by Steve Brodner at the MoCCA Art Fest.

Special Preview of GERONIMO STILTON Graphic Novel #11 "We'll Always Have Paris"!

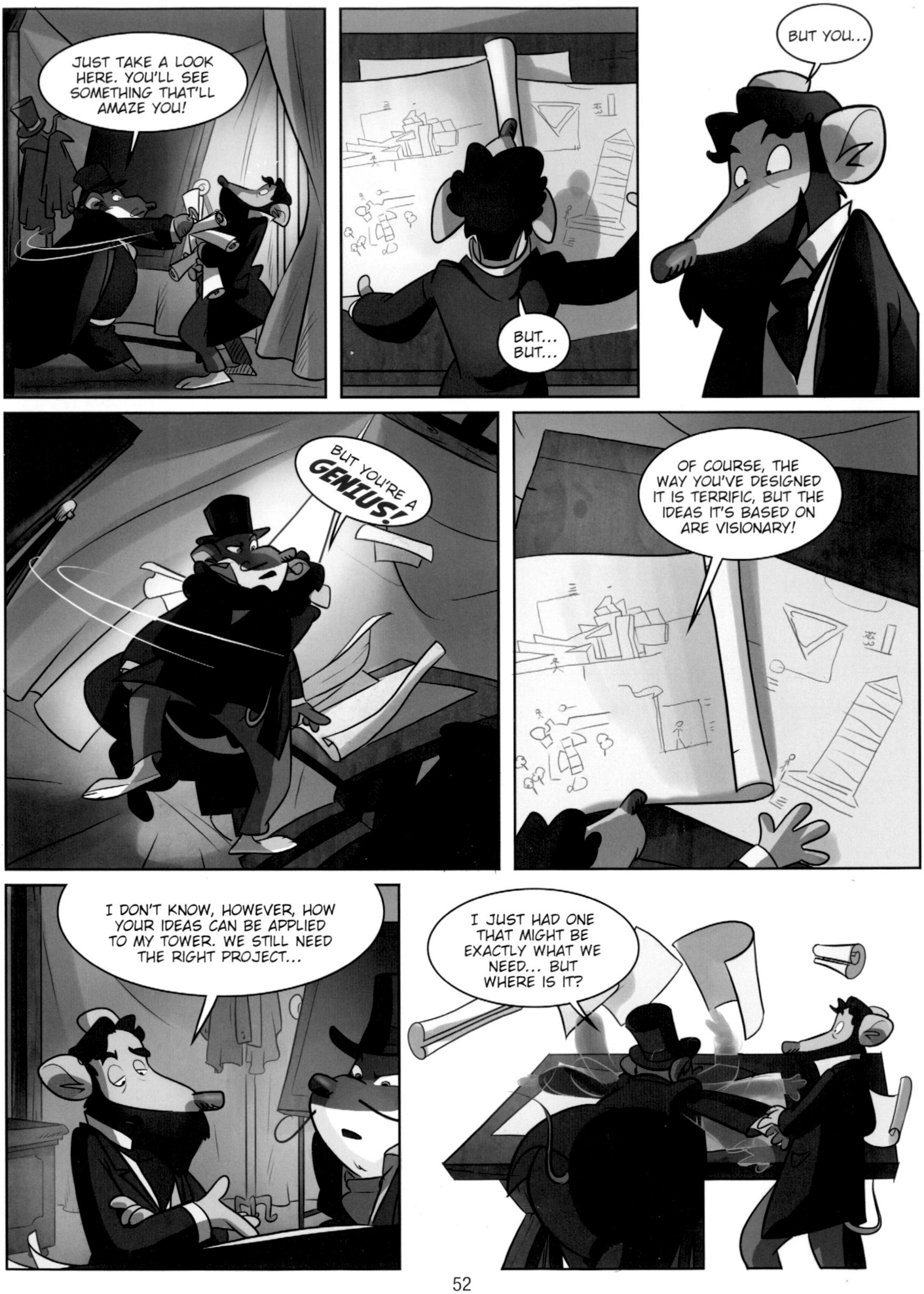

JUST TAKE A LOOK HERE. YOU'LL SEE SOMETHING THAT'LL AMAZE YOU!
BUT... BUT...
BUT YOU...
BUT YOU'RE A GENIUS!
OF COURSE, THE WAY YOU'VE DESIGNED IT IS TERRIFIC, BUT THE IDEAS IT'S BASED ON ARE VISIONARY!
I DON'T KNOW, HOWEVER, HOW YOUR IDEAS CAN BE APPLIED TO MY TOWER. WE STILL NEED THE RIGHT PROJECT...
I JUST HAD ONE THAT MIGHT BE EXACTLY WHAT WE NEED... BUT WHERE IS IT?

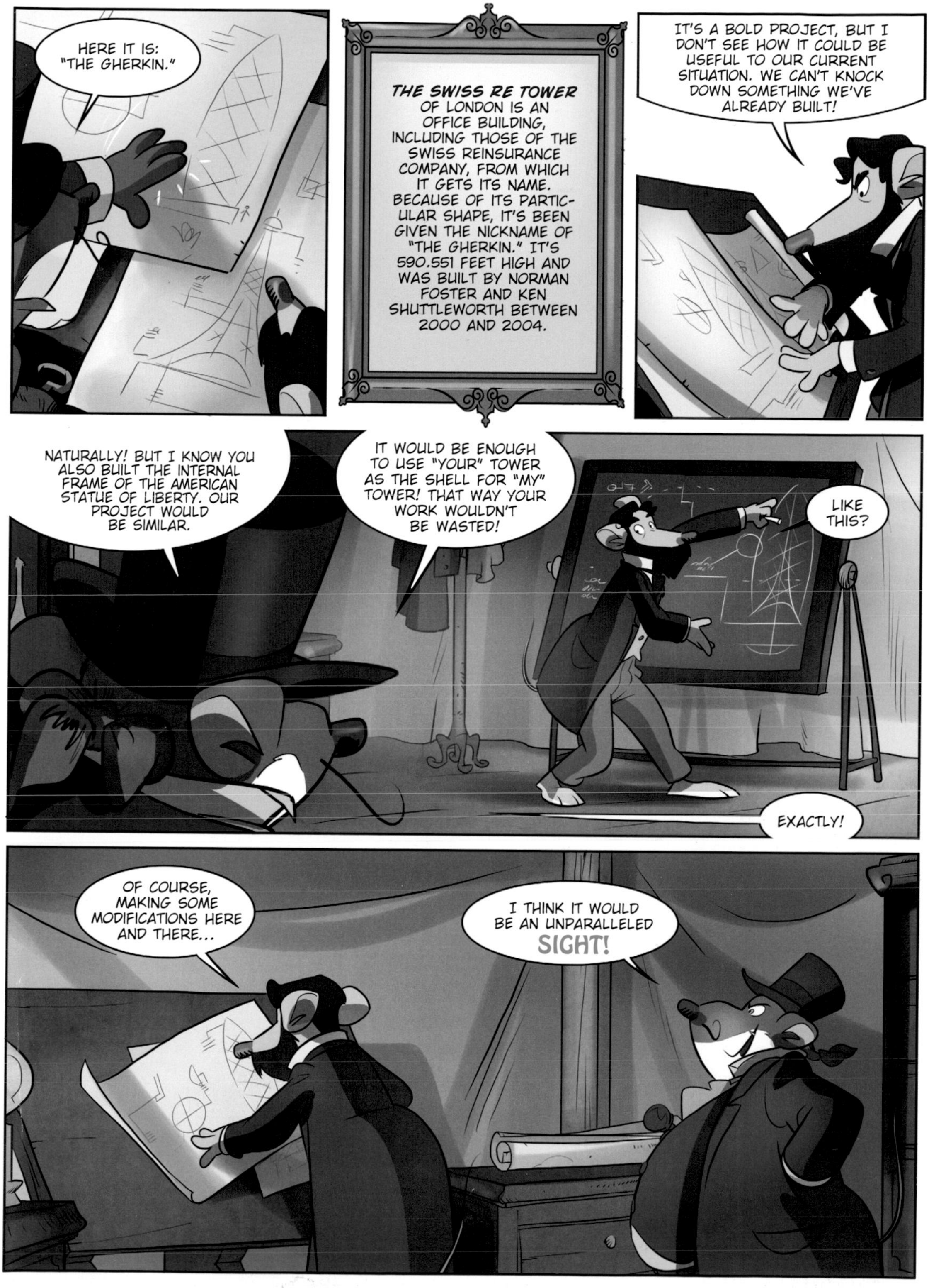
HERE IT IS: "THE GHERKIN."
THE SWISS RE TOWER OF LONDON IS AN OFFICE BUILDING, INCLUDING THOSE OF THE SWISS REINSURANCE COMPANY, FROM WHICH IT GETS ITS NAME. BECAUSE OF ITS PARTICULAR SHAPE, IT'S BEEN GIVEN THE NICKNAME OF "THE GHERKIN." IT'S 590.551 FEET HIGH AND WAS BUILT BY NORMAN FOSTER AND KEN SHUTTLEWORTH BETWEEN 2000 AND 2004.
IT'S A BOLD PROJECT, BUT I DON'T SEE HOW IT COULD BE USEFUL TO OUR CURRENT SITUATION. WE CAN'T KNOCK DOWN SOMETHING WE'VE ALREADY BUILT!
NATURALLY! BUT I KNOW YOU ALSO BUILT THE INTERNAL FRAME OF THE AMERICAN STATUE OF LIBERTY. OUR PROJECT WOULD BE SIMILAR.
IT WOULD BE ENOUGH TO USE "YOUR" TOWER AS THE SHELL FOR "MY" TOWER! THAT WAY YOUR WORK WOULDN'T BE WASTED!
LIKE THIS?
EXACTLY!
OF COURSE, MAKING SOME MODIFICATIONS HERE AND THERE...
I THINK IT WOULD BE AN UNPARALLELED SIGHT!

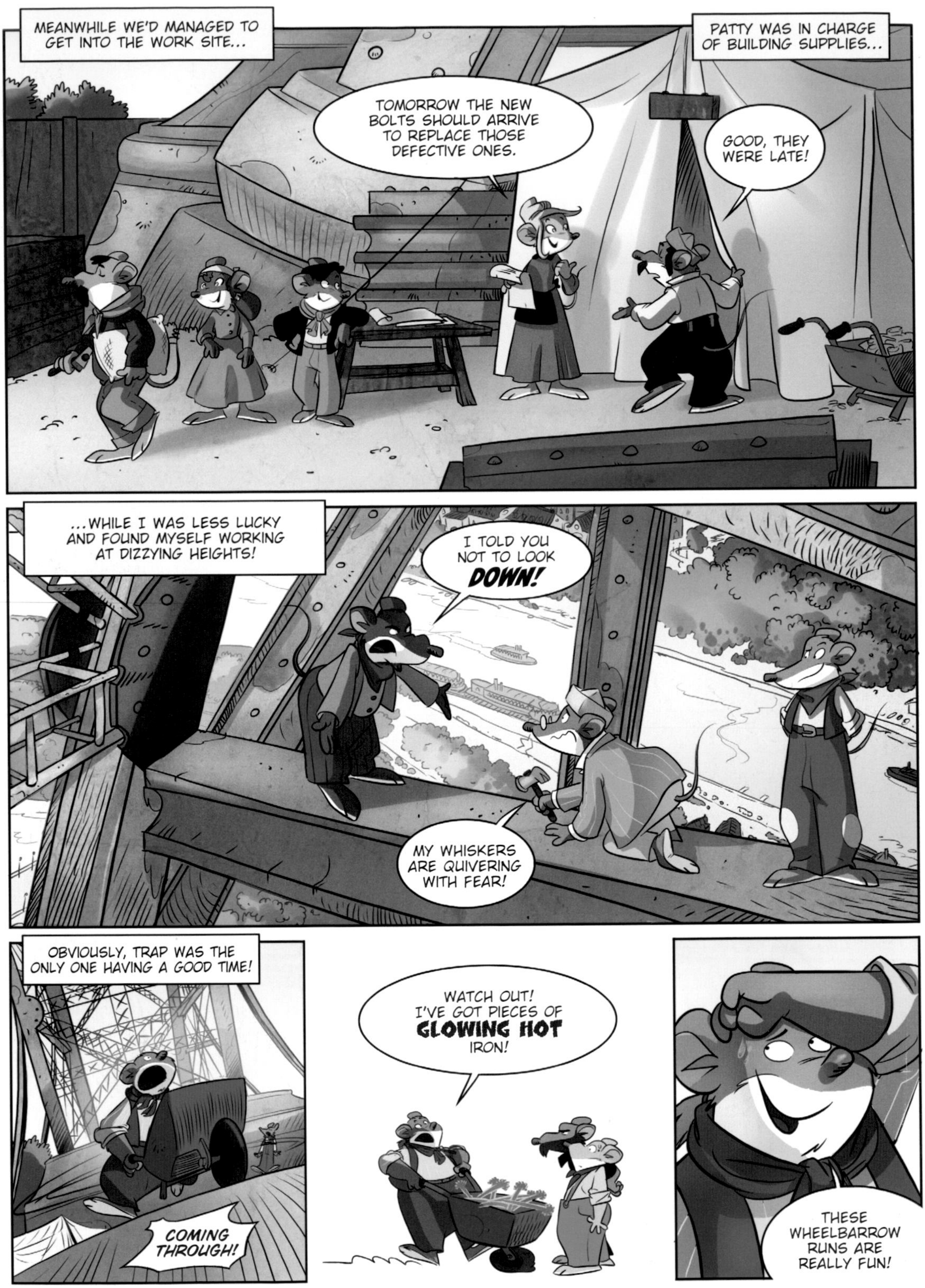
MEANWHILE WE'D MANAGED TO GET INTO THE WORK SITE...
PATTY WAS IN CHARGE OF BUILDING SUPPLIES...
TOMORROW THE NEW BOLTS SHOULD ARRIVE TO REPLACE THOSE DEFECTIVE ONES.
GOOD, THEY WERE LATE!
...WHILE I WAS LESS LUCKY AND FOUND MYSELF WORKING AT DIZZYING HEIGHTS!
I TOLD YOU NOT TO LOOK DOWN!
MY WHISKERS ARE QUIVERING WITH FEAR!
OBVIOUSLY, TRAP WAS THE ONLY ONE HAVING A GOOD TIME!
COMING THROUGH!
WATCH OUT! I'VE GOT PIECES OF GLOWING HOT IRON!
THESE WHEELBARROW RUNS ARE REALLY FUN!

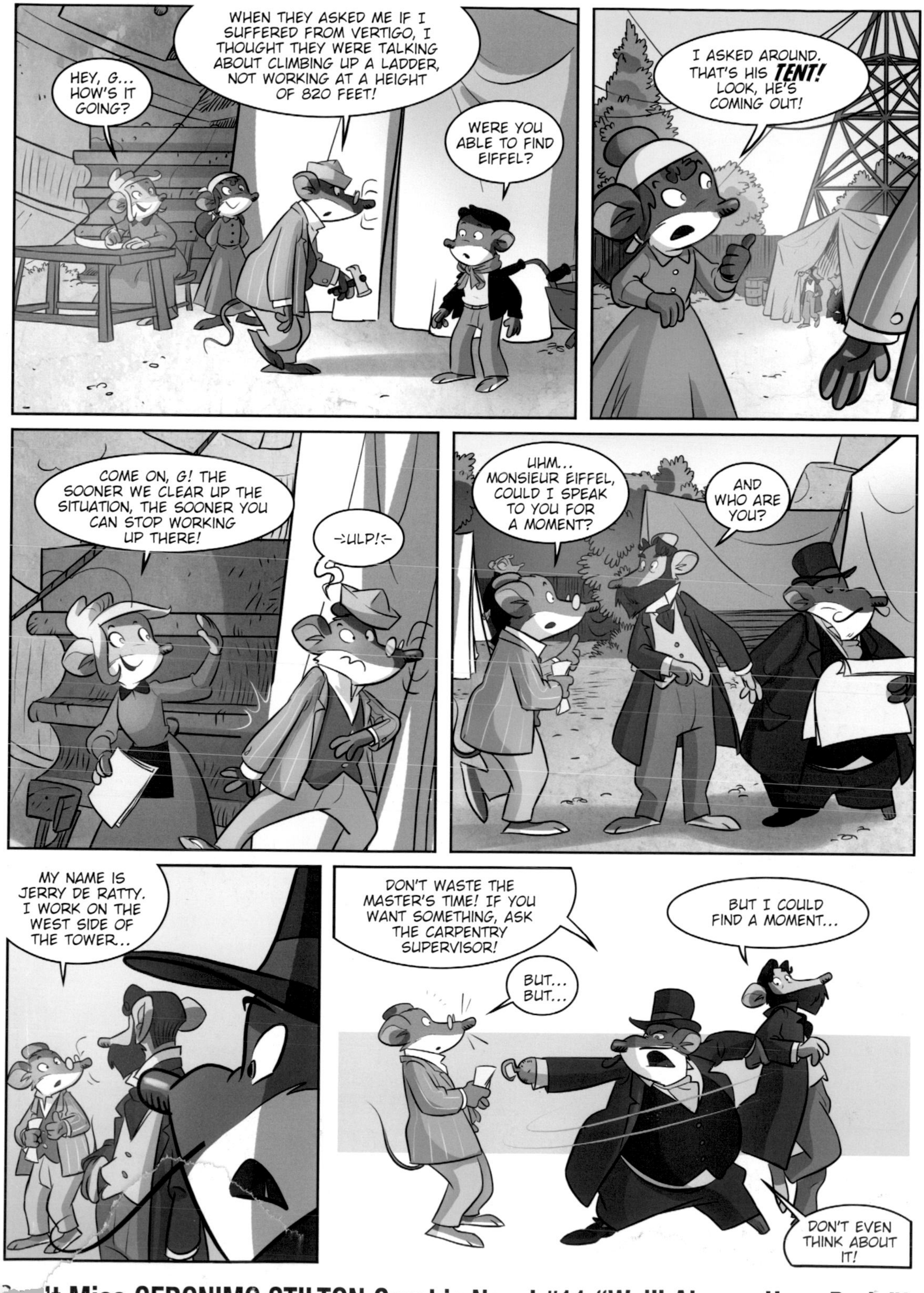
HEY, G... HOW'S IT GOING?
WHEN THEY ASKED ME IF I SUFFERED FROM VERTIGO, I THOUGHT THEY WERE TALKING ABOUT CLIMBING UP A LADDER, NOT WORKING AT A HEIGHT OF 820 FEET!
WERE YOU ABLE TO FIND EIFFEL?
I ASKED AROUND. THAT'S HIS TENT! LOOK, HE'S COMING OUT!
COME ON, G! THE SOONER WE CLEAR UP THE SITUATION, THE SOONER YOU CAN STOP WORKING UP THERE!
ULP!
UHM... MONSIEUR EIFFEL, COULD I SPEAK TO YOU FOR A MOMENT?
AND WHO ARE YOU?
MY NAME IS JERRY DE RATTY. I WORK ON THE WEST SIDE OF THE TOWER...
DON'T WASTE THE MASTER'S TIME! IF YOU WANT SOMETHING, ASK THE CARPENTRY SUPERVISOR!
BUT... BUT...
BUT I COULD FIND A MOMENT...
DON'T EVEN THINK ABOUT IT!

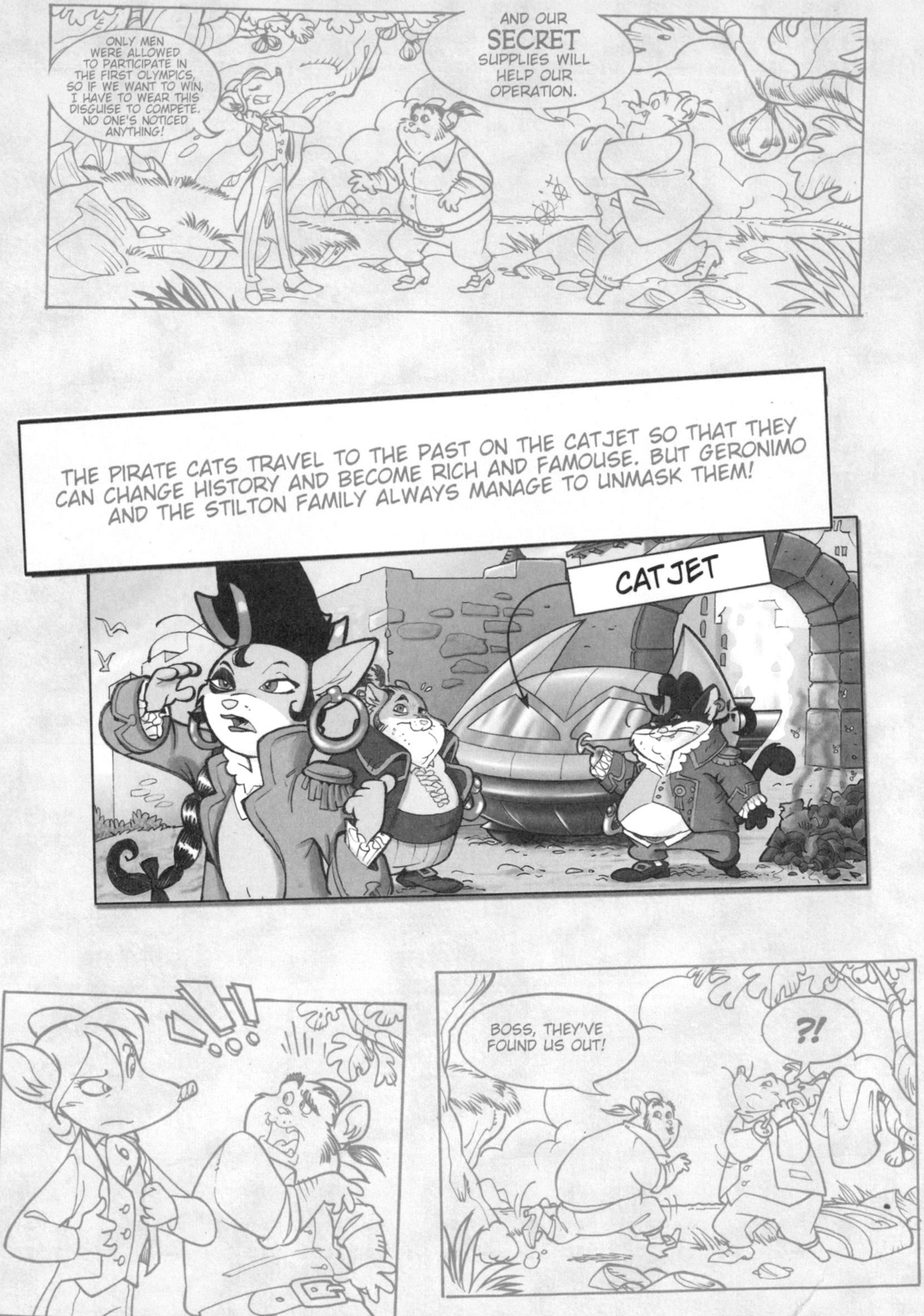
ONLY MEN WERE ALLOWED TO PARTICIPATE IN THE FIRST OLYMPICS, SO IF WE WANT TO WIN, I HAVE TO WEAR THIS DISGUISE TO COMPETE. NO ONE'S NOTICED ANYTHING!
AND OUR SECRET SUPPLIES WILL HELP OUR OPERATION.
THE PIRATE CATS TRAVEL TO THE PAST ON THE CATJET SO THAT THEY CAN CHANGE HISTORY AND BECOME RICH AND FAMOUSE. BUT GERONIMO AND THE STILTON FAMILY ALWAYS MANAGE TO UNMASK THEM!
CATJET
!!!
BOSS, THEY'VE FOUND US OUT!
?!